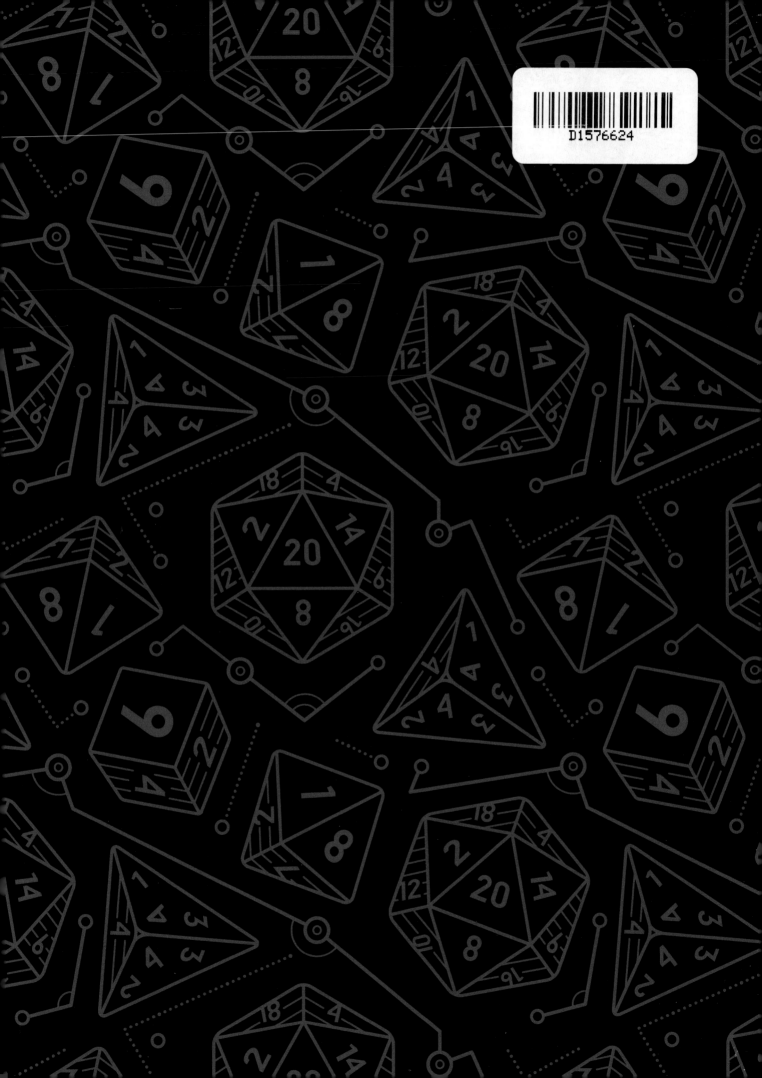

Farshore

First published in Great Britain 2021 by Farshore
An imprint of HarperCollins*Publishers*
1 London Bridge Street, London SE1 9GF
www.farshore.co.uk

HarperCollins*Publishers*
1st Floor, Watermarque Building, Ringsend Road
Dublin 4, Ireland

Written by Susie Rae
Edited by Craig Jelley
Designed by Nick Avery
Cover design by John Stuckey

This book features illustrations by Julian Kok Joon Wen, David René Christensen, Brian Valeza, Ben Wootten, Mark Behm, Caroline Gariba, Zuzanna Wużyk, Andrew Mar, Sidharth Chaturvedi, Cory Trego-Erdner, Jesper Ejsing, Tyler Walpole, Filip Burburan, Zoltan Boros, Scott Murphy, Christopher Burdett, Jason Juta, Robson Michel, Kieran Yanner, Craig J Spearing, E.W. Hekaton, Kekai Kotaki, Jon Hodgson, Titus Lunter, Svetlin Velinov, Randy Gallegos, Lake Hurwitz, Richard Whitters, Justin Sweet, Conceptopolis, Shawn Wood, Marcela Medeiros, Christopher Moeller, Steve Prescott, Stacey Allan, Alessandra Pisano, Brynn Metheney, Irina Nordsol, Autumn Rain Turkel, John Stanko, Daniel Landerman, Franz Vohwinkel, Beth Trott, Raoul Vitale, Jared Blando, Justin Gerard, Aaron Hübrich, E.M. Gist, Emrah Elmasli, Michael Berube, Zack Stella, Min Yum, Hector Ortiz, Lars Grant-West, Dave Dorman, William O'Connor, Alex Stone, Daren Bader, Tomas Giorello, Aleksi Briclot, Adam Paquette, Eric Belisle, Jedd Chevrier, Ilya Shkipin, Allen Douglas, Chris Seaman, Wayne England, Tom Babbey, Cynthia Sheppard, Rob Rey, Grzegorz Rutkowski, Mike Schley.

ISBN 978 0 7555 0109 0
Printed in Romania
001

Stay safe online. Farshore is not responsible for content hosted by third parties.

Farshore takes its responsibility to the planet and its inhabitants very seriously.
We aim to use papers from well-managed forests run by responsible suppliers.

MIX
Paper from
responsible sources
FSC™ C007454

This book is produced from independently certified FSC™ paper
to ensure responsible forest management.

For more information visit: www.harpercollins.co.uk/green

DUNGEONS & DRAGONS®

ANNUAL 2022

CONTENTS

INTRODUCTION

For almost 50 years, DUNGEONS & DRAGONS fans have gathered around their gaming tables, dice in hand, ready to explore the exciting and elaborate fantasy worlds presided over by their Dungeon Masters.

Today, the game is bigger than ever, with millions of players worldwide. No matter how you want to play – are you a character-driven storyteller or a hardcore mechanics nerd on the hunt for new directions to take your gameplay in? – there will be endless campaigns, characters and communities to match your style.

So where to start? Dive into this annual to discover fascinating lore from D&D's rich history, tips and tricks to bring to the table, challenging activities to test your wisdom and intelligence, and the newest campaigns and content from Wizards of the Coast and the many brilliant podcasters, streamers and communities who play D&D around the globe.

SO ROLL UP YOUR CHARACTER, GRAB YOUR DICE AND LET'S GET STARTED!

EXPLORING ELVES

The people of the Forgotten Realms are as diverse as they are fascinating. There are countless societies, tribes, clans and factions, all with their own cultures, beliefs and ways of living. Gone are the stereotypes of haughty elves and curmudgeonly dwarves – your options are endless!

HIGH ELVES

Originating from the Feywild, or faerie realm, high elves are often drawn to woodlands. Though many of these elves live solitary existences, many display a love for the finer things in life, so it isn't uncommon to find them among other peoples in populous settlements. Straddling the boundary between the Feywild and the Forgotten Realms, high elves have been known to travel freely between the two.

SPECIAL SKILLS:
High elves are often highly intelligent and are adept at some magics, particularly types that relate to nature.

KEY CLASSES:
Due to their increased Intelligence, high elves make excellent wizards.

DID YOU KNOW?
The magic in high elves' blood sometimes gives their skin a bronze or blue-white hue.

WOOD ELVES

The most common type of elf, wood elves love nature. They are typically found in tight-knit woodland communities and often form bonds with local fauna. Though they aren't naturally drawn to magic, preferring bows and longswords, it isn't uncommon to find wood elves who become sorcerers, druids and even bards.

SPECIAL SKILLS:
Their close connection to nature means that wood elves can move swiftly and stealthily through the forest.

KEY CLASSES:
Wood elves are often high in Wisdom, which can lend itself to the Druid, Cleric, and Ranger classes.

DID YOU KNOW?
Most elves do not need to sleep, instead going into a meditation-like trance when they want to rest up.

THE REALM

DROW

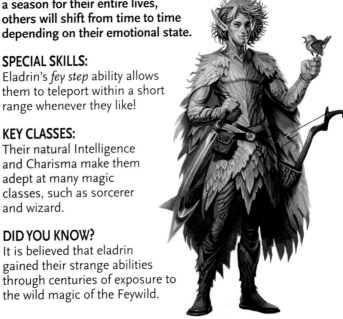

Though drow, sometimes known as dark elves, can usually be found in the Underdark, many individuals and even full tribes of drow have escaped the shadowy realm and created secretive settlements across Faerûn. As they are sensitive to the sun, you're most likely to find them in places with less direct sunlight.

SPECIAL SKILLS:
Due to their subterranean ancestry, drow have incredible *darkvision* – better than almost any creature – and can summon *faerie fire* to light the way.

KEY CLASSES:
These charismatic elves can make powerful bards, warlocks and sorcerers.

DID YOU KNOW?
One of the most famous drow is the legendary ranger and hero Drizzt Do'Urden.

ELADRIN

These mysterious elves, native to the Feywild, have a deep attachment to the seasons. Their temperament and skills stem from the season they are currently embodying – peaceful autumn, pensive winter, cheerful spring and bold summer. While some embody a season for their entire lives, others will shift from time to time depending on their emotional state.

SPECIAL SKILLS:
Eladrin's *fey step* ability allows them to teleport within a short range whenever they like!

KEY CLASSES:
Their natural Intelligence and Charisma make them adept at many magic classes, such as sorcerer and wizard.

DID YOU KNOW?
It is believed that eladrin gained their strange abilities through centuries of exposure to the wild magic of the Feywild.

OTHER PEOPLES

ROCK & FOREST GNOMES
The most common types of gnome, forest gnomes, as you might imagine, favour the flora of the woodlands, while rock gnomes have a knack for tinkering that makes them adept artificers.

LIGHTFOOT & STOUT HALFLINGS
Overlook these diminutive folk at your own risk! Lightfoot halflings are swift and nimble, while stout halflings, who are sometimes suspected of containing dwarven blood, can be surprisingly strong and resilient.

MOUNTAIN DWARVES & DUERGAR
Like drow, duergar originate from the Underdark, while mountain dwarves often live deep within mountains. Both have a skilful knowledge of stoneworking.

ACROSS FAERÛN

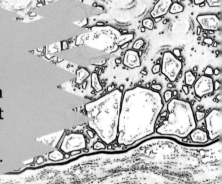

ICEWIND DALE

Only the hardiest adventurers make their way to Icewind Dale in the northerly reaches of Faerûn. Those who do will be faced with frigid winds, barren landscapes, and the kind of people that don't want to be found. Still, if you dare to brave the chilly climes, you may discover some beautiful locations and fascinating creatures. Remember to wrap up warm!

CREATURES OF ICEWIND DALE

SNOWY OWLBEAR

Part owl, part bear, owlbears can be found all over the Realms – but the snowy ones can only be found in the wilds of Icewind Dale.

FROST GIANT

Giants come in many forms, but the most common in the Dale are frost giants. They sometimes turn into polar werebears – a frightening sight for any adventurer!

YETI

Everyone knows the story of the yeti; bear-like creatures that prowl frozen landscapes. If you're brave enough to take one on, be sure not to look them in the eye, as their gaze can paralyse you.

ICE MEPHIT

These small, nasty creatures travelled to the Material Plane from other elemental planes. They can be found in swarms and can overpower an unsuspecting party of adventurers.

TEN TOWNS

Most of the people hardy enough to make their home in Icewind Dale live in the small collection of frontier villages known as the Ten Towns. Though the locals tend to be fairly independent by nature, co-operation between these towns is key for survival in such a hostile landscape.

Ten-

The Redrun

KELVIN'S CAIRN

The only mountain within a thousand miles, the icy peak of Kelvin's Cairn towers over the landscape of Icewind Dale. It is surrounded by the Dwarven Valley, which is almost as deep as the Cairn is tall, and has been home to the dwarves of Clan Battlehammer for generations.

FIELDS OF SLAUGHTER

This barren stretch of land, which runs between the Spine of the World mountain range and the elven fortress known as the Severed Hand, got its name from a great battle that took place there. Legend says that so much blood was spilled that day, the fields were stained red for months afterwards.

Kelvin's Cairn

Lonelywood

Termalaine

Maer Dualdon

Caer-Konig

Lac Dinneshere

BRYN SHANDER

Bryn Shander is the capital of Icewind Dale, insomuch as a place like Icewind Dale can have a capital. Located at the top of a hill, it is the biggest of the Ten Towns and is considered to be the centre of trade and military defence in the area.

...men

Caer-Dineval

Bryn Shander

Targos

The Eastway

rns

Good Mead

Easthaven

LAC DINNESHERE

Icewind Dale is home to three lakes so cold that a few seconds submerged in their waters could kill you: Maer Dualdon, Lac Dinneshere and Redwaters. Many legends surround the eerie banks of Lac Dinneshere, including the tale of a ghostly White Lady who haunts its shores.

Dougan's Hole

Redwaters

Ten Trail

CAMPAIGN

RIME OF THE FROSTMAIDEN

Adventure is a dish best served cold, as you'll discover in this chilly campaign. The frozen land of Icewind Dale has fallen under the curse of the evil goddess Auril, also known as the Frostmaiden, who has plunged the land into almost-constant darkness.

WHERE TO START?

A campaign for levels 1-13, *Rime of the Frostmaiden* starts you off easy. There are a couple of different starting quest options, which will lead you into a sandbox-like section of the campaign, with plenty of smaller side-quests to help new players explore the world while finding their feet and levelling up.

SECRETS AND TALL TALES

Rumours and secrets are a major part of the campaign. Players can unlock a table of Tall Tales, which the DM can drop into game to help the party towards their end goal. Each character also starts out with a Character Secret, such as escaped prisoners, secret doppelgangers or players with a clandestine quest to fulfil.

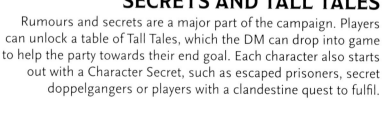

SPOTLIGHT

AURIL THE FROSTMAIDEN

Unlike your standard RPG boss, the wrathful ice goddess Auril takes on many forms and must be defeated not once, but three times, once in each of her forms: the Cold Crone, the Brittle Maiden, and the Queen of Frozen Tears.

NEW RULES

The source book contains new sets of rules for different encounters and mini-games, including ice-fishing, dogsledding, and surviving Frigid Water and Extreme Cold.

THREE KOBOLDS IN A TRENCHCOAT

Among dozens of new and exciting stat-blocks (including snowy owlbears, dwarf mindflayers, and mechanical dragons), *Rime of the Frostmaiden* finally brings a long-requested and oft-homebrewed classic to the D&D canon: three kobolds in a trenchcoat!

LOCATIONS

TEN TOWNS

The campaign starts in the Ten Towns, a collection of small frontier towns in the frigid land of Icewind Dale.

SUNBLIGHT

This Duergar fortress, built into the mountains surrounding Ten Towns, presents a fun dungeon to explore early on in the campaign.

NGEON CRAWL

party ventures toward the lair of Acererak the
ut the way is paved with deadly traps. The safest
can be found by following this pattern of paving
s, moving in any direction except diagonally.
your party to a showdown with the lich.

PAVING STONES KEY

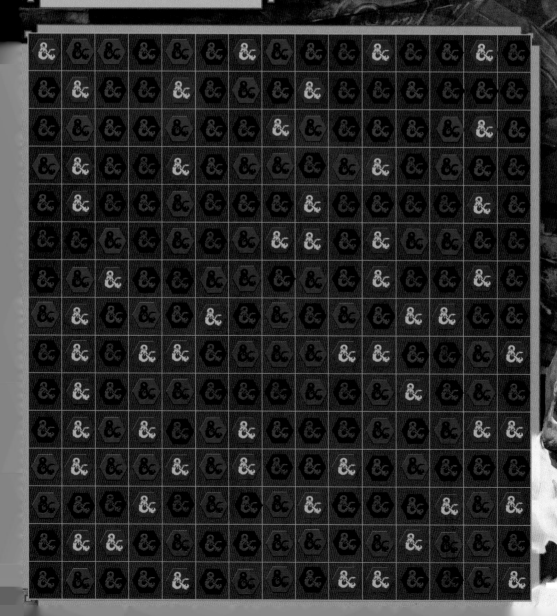

ESCAPE FROM CASTLE RAVENLOFT

Count Strahd von Zarovich has taken a group of innocents captive, and it's up to you to rescue them. Make your way through the maze, collecting the prisoners on the way, and avoiding the dark lord himself.

ANSWERS ON PAGES 92-93

BEYOND THE

DARK ALLIANCE

The magical crystal shard, Crenshinibon, has been lost in Icewind Dale. Now, in this explosive action RPG video game, legions of villains, monsters and armies are flocking to the frozen region to seek its power, and our heroes are the only thing that stands in their way.

CHOOSE YOUR HERO

You can play as one of four iconic heroes: drow ranger Drizzt Do'Urden, human barbarian Wulfgar, dwarf fighter Bruenor Battlehammer or human fighter Cattie-Brie. Each character has their own unique playstyle and customisable abilities, earning ever more powerful gear and unlocking new skills as you play.

FIGHT ALONGSIDE YOUR FRIENDS

The joy of *Dark Alliance* is that, much like D&D, you can play co-op with your friends. Pick a hero each, then settle in to unleash devastating combos to topple dangerous monsters too powerful to take on alone.

THE CRYSTAL SHARD

The game is set straight after R.A. Salvatore's first novel, which saw Drizzt and his companions battle a dark mage over a powerful magical artifact called Crenshinibon, or the crystal shard. Crenshinibon thirsts for ever greater power and will warp the minds of those who wield it.

TABLETOP

CONQUER UNSTOPPABLE MONSTERS

The game has no shortage of monsters for you to fight, straight from the D&D lore that you know and love. Face enormous frost giants, terrifying beholders, ghostly liches, and, yes, the inevitable dragons, as you and your heroes battle to protect Icewind Dale from Crenshinibon and the hordes of villains that have fallen under the shard's thrall.

KELVIN

Hardcore D&D fans might be familiar with Kelvin's Cairn, the tallest (and only) mountain in Icewind Dale. Well, now you have the opportunity to meet – and fight – its namesake: Kelvin the mighty frost giant.

BRAVE THE FROZEN LANDSCAPE

Dark Alliance allows you to explore the world of Icewind Dale like never before. Climb Kelvin's Cairn, venture into frozen caves, and bask in the terrifying beauty of the iconic landscape as you defend your homeland from armies of abominable monsters.

DRIZZT DO'URDEN

It's hard to go far in the Forgotten Realms without hearing the name of legendary drow ranger Drizzt Do'Urden. Born in the shadowy Underdark city of Menzoberranzan, Drizzt left his home for the surface, where he became one of the greatest heroes in Faerûn history.

LEAVING MENZOBERRANZAN

Though he may not be the only resident of Menzoberranzan to question the violent culture that existed under the control of spider goddess Lolth, Drizzt was the first person to risk his life to leave the city.

LOLTH

The spider goddess's dark power cast a shadow over the whole of Menzoberranzan, which prompted Drizzt to leave the city for good. Naturally, Lolth wasn't happy about his departure, and Drizzt's life on the surface is plagued by clerics of Lolth, who seek to destroy him.

THE HUNTER

When faced with extreme danger, Drizzt is sometimes taken over by a wild, animalistic alter-ego: The Hunter. True to his name, the Hunter has heightened senses and an almost unnatural fighting ability, but is prone to losing control in battle.

GUENHWYVAR

Drizzt is rarely seen without his animal companion, a black panther by the name of Guenhwyvar. Guen actually lives on the Astral plane, and can be summoned to Drizzt's side using a magical onyx figurine.

ARTEMIS ENTERERI

Aside from the sinister clerics of Lolth, Drizzt's greatest nemesis is a bloodthirsty human assassin, Artemis Entereri. After kidnapping and threatening Drizzt's friends, Artemis found himself an enemy for life.

THE COMPANIONS OF THE HALL

Despite appearances, Drizzt is not always a solitary hunter. He is part of legendary adventuring group, the Companions of the Hall, named after the dwarven fortress, Mithral Hall.

CATTI-BRIE

Talented human fighter Catti-Brie is lethal with a bow and arrow, but her kind heart means that she will often pursue non-violence whenever it's possible.

WULFGAR

Hailing from Icewind Dale, Wulfgar is a hardy barbarian who worships the god of battle, Tempus, and honours him every time he swings his legendary battleaxe, Aegis-fang.

BRUENOR BATTLEHAMMER

Cattie-Brie and Wulfgar's adoptive father is Bruenor Battlehammer, a dwarven fighter and king of Mithral Hall. As well as being a fearsome warrior, Bruenor is a brilliant leader, beloved by his subjects.

REGIS

There's nothing that halfling rogue Regis wants more than a quiet life, lounging by the river and smoking a pipe. Unfortunately for him, he is constantly dragged into adventures and battles, alongside his loyal companions.

TALKING D&D: R.A. SALVATORE

Even if you're only just starting out in the world of D&D, it won't be long before you come across the handiwork of R.A. Salvatore. The author of more than 40 books set in the Forgotten Realms, Salvatore has created some of the most iconic characters, settings and events that DUNGEONS & DRAGONS fans know and love - including Icewind Dale, Menzoberranzan, and legendary drow ranger Drizzt Do'Urden.

STARTING OUT

R.A. Salvatore's writing career had an unlikely start. *"I was working in a plastics factory and as a bouncer,"* he tells us, *"and I was very bored, so I started writing a book in my head. I sent it to [publisher] TSR, and the editor looked at it and said 'we only have room for Forgotten Realms books. Can you set it in the Forgotten Realms?' This was the 80s, so there was no internet and no way of knowing what the Forgotten Realms were."* Still, he wrote an outline and got the job – the only catch was that he had to write the whole book in four months!

THE BIRTH OF DRIZZT DO'URDEN

Despite being one of the most iconic characters in D&D lore, Drizzt wasn't even in the original outline of his first book, *The Crystal Shard*. Salvatore explains: *"Wulfgar was going to be my main character. [My editor] told me she wanted a sidekick for Wulfgar. I told her I'd get back to her, and she said, 'No, I need it now. I'm late for a meeting.' So off the top of my head, I said, 'Ok. A dark elf. A drow ranger. No one's ever done that before.' I started writing the book and, two pages in, I had Drizzt running across the tundra and being ambushed by some yetis. And I realised this book wasn't about Wulfgar, it was Drizzt."*

CREATING THE DROW

Following the success of *The Crystal Shard*, Salvatore found there was a surprising amount of interest around his new character of Drizzt Do'Urden, and he was asked to write a backstory for the character. There was only one problem. *"Drizzt is a dark elf – a drow,"* he says. *"At the time, there were a few modules and a one-page entry in the* Fiend Folio *for the drow, and that was it."* Never one to shy away from a challenge, he not only wrote a backstory for Drizzt, but created a whole drow civilisation, Menzoberranzan, complete with a full history, political system, and religion.

BUILDING MENZOBERRANZAN

"When I was presented with the challenge of creating Menzoberranzan, I thought it should be the type of culture where everyone on the outside thinks they're just evil,' Salvatore explains. *"But that's ridiculous, because a society couldn't survive like that. There would be one person left. They have to have codes; they have to have a way of life. So I based it on* The Godfather *by Mario Puzo, and the five families of New York became the eight families of the drow. I guess I wrote* The Godmother."

BEYOND MENZO

In Salvatore's newest book, *Starlight Enclave,* we discover a drow tribe beyond Menzoberranzan. The aevendrow live on a glacier in the far north of Faerûn, beyond Icewind Dale. Very different from the drow of the Underdark, Salvatore describes the aevendrow as *"a Renaissance world, with parts of it being based on Florence, in Italy".* *"This is an egalitarian, council-ruled city, where all of their needs are met by the glacier, and the crops that grow and the streams that flow,"* he explains. *"They're post-competitive, but they're still very competitive. They have sports. The biggest battle scene in the book is a cross between American football, soccer, and rugby, based on a game that has been played once a year in Florence since about the sixteenth century. It's beautiful and brutal."*

SOCIETIES THAT MAKE SENSE

Why the new drow tribes? Well, Salvatore wants to show the diversity of the drow race, and overcome some common misconceptions. *"The drow aren't evil. It's Lolth [the drider goddess that Menzoberranzan society revolves around]. Menzoberranzan is a good society being corrupted by a few bad players. Drizzt wasn't unique in disliking this culture, he was just the first to act on it by leaving the city. So you have to show other societies of the drow who weren't corrupted by Lolth. I love building societies that make sense."* So should we be excited for this new drow society? Salvatore certainly thinks so: *"Anyone who reads this book is going to want to have adventures up there."*

PLAYING FAVOURITES

Does R.A. Salvatore have favourites of the characters he's created? *"I have favourites, but fortunately it changes. When I focus on a different character, I start to appreciate them more. In the new book, there are a few new, distinct characters of the aevendrow, and I know my favourite out of the gate – Azzudonna, one of the fighters. I love the others, but she's my favourite."*

WHAT'S NEXT?

So what's next for R.A. Salvatore in the D&D world? *"This trilogy may be the last thing I write in the Forgotten Realms,"* he says. *"I might have said everything I need to say about the world. But I said that after the first book, and that was almost forty years ago!"*

STARTING POINT

If you want to explore the characters and societies created by R.A. Salvatore, there are dozens to choose from. Why not start with his first Forgotten Realms book, *The Crystal Shard*?

MENZOBERRANZAN

Menzoberranzan, sometimes called the 'City of Spiders', is one of the best-known cities in the Underdark, a massive network of tunnels, caverns, and settlements that exists beneath much of Faerûn. It was founded by worshippers of the goddess Lolth, and for centuries was mostly home to drow. However, now people from many walks of life call it home … whether they like it or not.

CREATURES OF THE UNDERDARK

MIND FLAYERS

You don't want to come across one of these creatures in the caverns of the Underdark. Mind flayers feed on their victims' brains, and have psionic powers that allow them to incapacitate those that cross them.

BEHOLDERS

Made up of a giant, floating eyeball with ten more eyes on stalks, it's near impossible to sneak up on a beholder. Each eye shoots a different magical ray, and their central eye omits an area of antimagic, disempowering any mages in the vicinity.

INTELLECT DEVOURERS

Resembling faceless brains on legs, intellect devourers are created by mindflayers from the brains of their victims and kept as servants. They can take over the bodies of their victims for several days, until the body starts to decay.

DRIDERS

Similar to centaurs, but creepier, driders have the upper half of a humanoid … and the body and legs of a giant spider. Originally created by Lolth as a punishment for disloyal drow, they can shoot webs and climb cavern walls, as well as cast spells and wield weapons!

MENZO LOCALES

TIER BRECHE

The cavern of Tier Breche houses the Academy of Menzoberranzan, a prestigious institution that schools clerics of Lolth, fighters, and wizards. The Academy is carved into the rock of the cavern itself, and is protected by magical defences, including two enormous, magically-animated spider statues.

THE BAZAAR

If you can think of it, you can probably buy it in the Bazaar ... if you know who to ask. Local law states that no permanent structures can be built here, and businesses are constantly moving around, which means tracking down a specific stallholder is easier said than done.

THE BRAERYN

Sometimes called 'Stenchstreets', the Braeryn probably isn't somewhere you'd go if you could avoid it. Home to only the poorest and most wretched inhabitants of Menzoberranzan, this may be a good place to go if you never want to be found.

QU'ELLARZ'ORL

This plateau is home to some of the most powerful drow houses in the city – and the ruins of defeated houses, left in place to serve as a reminder to others. Qu'ellarz'orl is separated from the crowds of Menzoberranzan by a field of giant mushrooms.

LAKE DONIGARTEN

Unbeknown to most, the dark waters of this subterranean lake hide a flooded, abandoned temple to Ghaunadaur, the strange and chaotic god of abominations.

COMMON FOES

Before you're ready to take on a tarrasque, duel a dragon, or battle a balor, your party needs to train up! Even the most eager Level 1 party needs to start somewhere, so why not try your hand in combat with some of these common monsters before you take on the next 'Big Bad'?

STIRGES

CHALLENGE RATING: 1/8

Stirges are basically oversized, bird-like mosquitoes – and they're out for blood. One stirge is little more than a pest, but a swarm of them attacking at once can be very dangerous if you're caught unawares.

GOBLINS

CHALLENGE RATING: 1/4

These diminutive humanoids can be found all over, from city settings to woodlands and underground caves. With only 7 hit points each, it's not difficult to take out one goblin – but watch your back, because they usually attack in large numbers.

KOBOLDS

CHALLENGE RATING: 1/8

Watch out below! Kobolds are small, reptilian creatures usually found in underground dungeons. You will rarely find a lone kobold – they live and hunt in packs. They often act as minions for their much larger distant relatives, dragons.

CHALLENGE RATINGS

Every creature in D&D fifth edition has a Challenge Rating. This is based on the level that a four- or five-person party would need to be in order to comfortably defeat this creature. So, a Level 1 party should be able to take on eight CR 1/8 monsters, but only one CR1 monster.

MIMICS
CHALLENGE RATING: 1/2

Look out! That tempting chest in the middle of a dungeon might not be what it seems. Mimics can take the form of almost any inanimate object, from chests to chairs, and lurk in wait for an oblivious victim.

HARPIES
CHALLENGE RATING: 1

Winged creatures with a woman's body and reptilian legs, harpies like to steal trinkets from their victims. If you're unlucky enough to hear the song of a harpy, you may become helplessly drawn towards the creature.

GNOLLS
CHALLENGE RATING: 1/2

Part hyena, part humanoid, gnolls are savage, feral creatures that live for the thrill of the hunt. They ambush their victims and, if you're really unlucky, feast on their flesh afterwards.

QUASITS
CHALLENGE RATING: 1

They may be small, but these demons can be vicious. They can turn invisible and shape-shift into a bat-like form, which, combined with their resistance to many types of damage, makes them very tricky to kill.

MANTICORES
CHALLENGE RATING: 3

With the body of a lion, head of a human, and wings of a dragon, manticores are a sight to behold. You don't want to get on the wrong side of their razor-sharp teeth, but be just as wary of their tail, which is covered in deadly spikes.

PODCASTS

Every year, more and more people are tuning in to podcasts to get their fix of D&D. Luckily, more and more games are being turned into podcasts to fulfil their audible needs. They span the gamut of the D&D world, from the Forgotten Realms to Eberron and beyond, and each is filled with a host of deep, often hilarious characters. Let's take a look at a few of these audio sensations.

HOW WE ROLL

How We Roll are a UK and Ireland based podcast featuring guests from all over the world. They started out playing horror RPG *Call of Cthulhu*, and love everything mystery, horror and suspense, but with a funny and heart-warming edge. They're known for their fast-paced games, beloved characters, and surprising twists in every tale they tell.

RIME OF THE FROSTMAIDEN

In the frozen wastes of Icewind Dale, an ancient evil has risen. Alongside their companions, the adventurers must discover they mystery that has kept Icewind Dale trapped in eternal winter.

Gann is a firbolg druid, who was born in the Icewind Dale tundra.

Graham, an amnesiac human rogue, awoke in a crashed ship.

Xalfiz the gnome artificer is served by a robotic penguin sidekick.

The gang are joined every week by some brilliant guest stars, including Daniel Kwan and DM Steve from the podcast *Asians Represent*; Sara (@mustangsart), the creator of the combat wheelchair; and *Rime of the Frostmaiden* writer Celeste Conowitch.

CURSE OF STRAHD

For over two years, *How We Roll* has been playing *Curse of Strahd*, set in the shadowy realm of Barovia, which is ruled over by the dark vampire lord, Strahd von Zarovich. Think you know the game? Think again – this campaign is filled with twists, turns ... and undead player characters! DM Joe Trier says this is one of his favourite modules to play: **"It's so sandboxy, with so much opportunity to customise and explore really interesting areas. It has some of the best set pieces, too."**

SESSION ZERO

DM Joe is a big fan of Session Zero, a pre-game session where the players and DM sit down to create their characters and discuss how they want the game to go. **"It starts with the GM saying, 'I've got an idea', then writing the initial NPCs and place based on that discussion. It's a nice place to talk about player expectations. Do you want lots of combat or roleplay? What level do you want to start at? How many magic items do you want?"**

THE ADVENTURE ZONE

If you're a fan of podcasts, there's a good chance you know the McElroy family already. *The Adventure Zone* is an actual play podcast from brothers Justin, Travis and Griffin, as well as their dad, Clint, in a variety of complex and hilarious homebrew settings.

BALANCE

The first *Adventure Zone* arc follows three unlikely adventurers who work for the enigmatic Bureau of Balance, tracking down seven mysterious and powerful relics across Faerûn and encountering mad scientists, a sadistic game show, a brilliant boy detective and a high-speed battle-cart race along the way.

Taako, the wise-cracking elf transmutation wizard, played by Justin, turned to a life of adventuring after a deadly accident brought an end to his career as a TV chef.

Magnus Burnsides is a human fighter, played by Travis. Gentle-hearted but impulsive, Magnus, along with his trusty axe Rail-splitter and his pet goldfish Steven, is the first to rush headlong into any situation.

Merle Highchurch, played by Clint, is a plant-loving dwarf cleric of the god Pan. After running away from his wife and children, it takes a series of adventures with a group of loveable goofballs to truly teach Merle the meaning of family.

GRADUATION

Hieronymous Wiggenstaff's School for Heroism and Villainy has trained the next generation of heroes and villains for hundreds of years. Graduation follows three students newly enrolled in the school's less-famous sidekick and henchman program.

Sir Fitzroy Maplecourt, played by Griffin, is a half-elf barbarian who was expelled from knight school after discovering a destructive affinity for wild magic. Together with his crab familiar, Snippers, he struggles to come to terms with his new magical abilities.

Argonaut 'Argo' Keene is a water genasi rogue, played by Clint. Cheerful, laid-back and loyal, Argo nonetheless struggles with self-doubt, and harbours a dark secret about why he came to the school in the first place.

The Firbolg, a nameless druid, played by Justin, came to the school after being forced to leave his clan. As he struggles to find his place in this strange new world, the Firbolg develops a surprising skill with accounting.

GRAPHIC NOVELS

If you love the podcast, you can enjoy the Balance arc in an awesome series of graphic novels – beginning with *Here There Be Gerblins* – illustrated by the super-talented Carey Pietsch.

AMNESTY

Besides D&D, the McElroys have ventured into other TTRPG systems. Their second full campaign, Amnesty, uses a game called *Monster of the Week*, and sees forest ranger Duck Newton, spell-slinging stage magician Aubrey Little and retired con-artist Ned Chicane encounter a series of strange cryptids who live among us, including Bigfoot and the Mothman.

EXPLAINING THE PLANES

The world of DUNGEONS & DRAGONS expands beyond the Forgotten Realms – sometimes onto different planes of existence. The planar system differs between games, depending on the Dungeon Master's masterplan, but there are dozens of different planes to explore.

THE PRIME MATERIAL PLANE

Most campaigns will take place in the Prime Material Plane. Existing at the very centre of many multiverses, it is the world of the majority of creatures in the world of D&D, from elves to dragons, and contains wildly varying climates, cultures, terrain, and levels of magics.

ECHOES OF THE MATERIAL PLANE

The Feywild

The Plane of Faerie, or the Feywild, exists in parallel to the Material Plane, and creatures can travel between them. It's home to many elves and is ruled by rival Summer and Winter Courts.

The Shadowfell

The Plane of Shadow exists as a twisted echo of the Material Plane. Occupied by dark magic and sinister creatures, the Shadowfell is avoided by all but the bravest adventurers – or most foolish.

THE TRANSITIVE PLANES

The Astral Plane

There are many ways to reach the endless silver sea of the Astral Plane, the plane of thoughts and dreams. Many can astral-project their consciousness from the Material Plane, while others may go there physically using a Plane Shift spell or plane-hopping colour pools.

The Ethereal Plane

This mist-shrouded dimension is frequented by ghosts that can move freely to the Material Plane and back. It is also plagued by ether cyclones, which can blow characters to another plane of existence entirely, or even hurl them, without warning, into the Astral Plane.

THE ELEMENTAL PLANES

The Plane of Fire

Those with passion in their hearts are drawn to the Plane of Fire and its glowing City of Brass. At its best, the plane is vibrant and exciting; at its worst, it represents destruction and chaos.

The Plane of Water

The Plane of Water represents the reliability of life and nature, embodying the duality of grief and healing. It is populated by shifting storms, that sometimes open portals on the seas of the Material Plane, drawing in unsuspecting ships.

The Plane of Air

This world is made up of interconnecting air streams known as the Labyrinth Winds. It embodies inspiration and change, but can be erratic and unreliable, changing on a whim.

The Plane of Earth

Made up of a chain of mountains, the capital city of the Plane of Earth is the City of Jewels, a dazzling place built entirely from precious gems. The opposite of the Plane of Air in many ways, it embodies stability and tradition.

THE ELEMENTAL CHAOS

Surrounding the Elemental Planes, where the elements begin to mix together, are areas of pure chaos. Though most elemental creatures avoid the Chaos, there is tell of strange hybrids that embody multiple elements at once.

THE OUTER PLANES

The Outer Planes are often occupied by gods and other deities. There are generally sixteen Outer Planes, corresponding with the eight alignments and the grey areas that exist between them. Mount Celestia, for example, represents Lawful Good, while the Nine Hells embody Lawful Evil.

THE FEYWILD

If you enter a particular magical pool or step into a mushroom circle, you might find yourself in the mysterious Plane of Faerie. This pocket dimension is a mirror of the Material Plane, filled with beautiful, unusual creatures, strange magic, and an eternal twilight that casts a gentle glow over the whole plane. Though it may be bright and full of wonder, travellers to the Feywilds must stay ever vigilant – things work very differently around here.

THE FEYDARK

Just as Faerûn has the Underdark, the Feywild has the Feydark, a maze of dark tunnels beneath the realms. Home to titans known as formordians, colourful magical mushrooms, and many other strange plants and creatures, the Feydark is very easy to get lost in – and very difficult to find your way out of – if you aren't familiar with its twists and turns.

SILDËYUIR

Home to the reclusive Star Elves, Sildëyuir was once a demiplane in its own right, but is now tucked away in the forests of the Feywild. Those who live here are peaceful people, who prefer to be left alone.

CREATURES OF THE FEYWILD

SATYRS

There's nothing satyrs love more than music and pleasure. These goat-legged humanoids are often found in the Feywild, and spend their days seeking out parties and celebrations. Be careful, though – these fun-loving creatures can easily charm you using their magical pan pipes.

DRYADS

Part woman, part tree, dryads are guardians of the forests. Each dryad is bonded to one specific tree, which serves as their life force, and the two can't be separated for long. Generally peaceful folk, the only way to ensure the wrath of a dryad is to harm or destroy a forest.

BLINK DOGS

Now you see them, now you don't! Blink dogs are strange canines who are named after their ability to blink in and out of the Material and Ethereal Planes. They are also highly intelligent and difficult to trick.

MEENLOCKS

Not all creatures in the Feywild are pleasant, and you definitely don't want to run into a meenlock on your travels. Created out of fear and horror, these sadistic creatures pick off travellers and use psychic abilities to torture their victims.

Plane of Water

Isle of Dread

Silt Flats

Swamp of Oblivion
(Plane of Ooze)

TIME IN THE FEYWILD
Due to the strange fey magic, time passes differently in the Feywild. Travellers there may find, on their return home, that what felt like days in the Feywild were actually weeks, months, or even years on the Material Plane.

FAE MAGIC
The magic in the Feywild is wild and unpredictable, which can have unexpected effects on outsiders who visit the realm. People often report hazy memories of their time there, and some sorcerers may find their usual magical skills are distorted.

Shadowfell

Material Plane

Feywild

The Furnaces

City of Jewels

Fountains of Creation
(Plane of Magma)

THE SUMMER AND GLOAMING COURTS
Most creatures in the Feywild are loyal to either the Summer or Gloaming Court. Those within the Summer Court – ruled by Titania – are known as the Seelie Fae, while those in the Gloaming Court – ruled by the Queen of Air and Darkness – are known as the Unseelie Fae. The two courts often find themselves at odds, and like to engage in weird yet playful contests in an attempt to best each other.

Fountains of Creation

Plane of Fire

VOLO'S (SCRAMBLED) GUIDE TO MONSTERS

Due to a misplaced spell, famed explorer Volo's notes on the monsters he's encountered on his travels have gotten scrambled up. Can you work out which creatures Volo came across on his most recent adventure?

8.

7.

1. SQUARE RAT

....

6.

2. ACTING LOUD

....

3. GRAND ROB ZONE

....

4.

4. GUARDED SPOON

....

3.

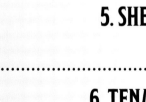

1.

5. SHEET KIP MOM

....

6. TENACIOUS BUGLE

....

2.

7. ROUGH EBBING TIMER

....

5.

8. BALD HUMMING SON

....

PACK IT IN

After spending the night camping out in Neverwinter Woods, the party have got their packs mixed up. Can you work out from the clues below which weapon, potion, and piece of equipment belongs to each adventurer?

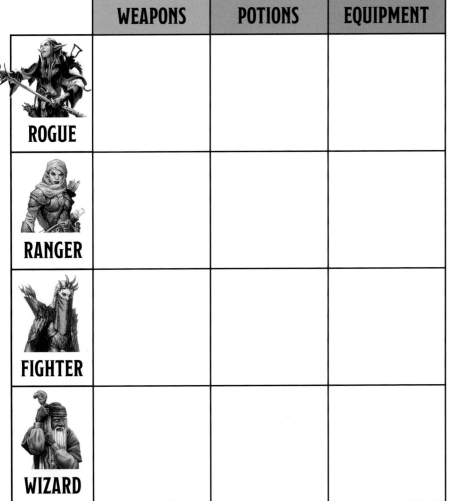

	WEAPONS	POTIONS	EQUIPMENT
ROGUE			
RANGER			
FIGHTER			
WIZARD			

CLUES

1. The wizard carries a longbow.
2. The rogue is less worried about healing than the wizard.
3. The rogue also fights with a ranged weapon.
4. The wizard can bring light to any room.
5. The fighter does not carry a sword.
6. The ranger carries a rope, but the fighter carries something to attach to it.
7. The oil of slipperiness and grappling iron belong to the same adventurer.
8. The remaining weapon, potion and equipment should be easy to assign now.

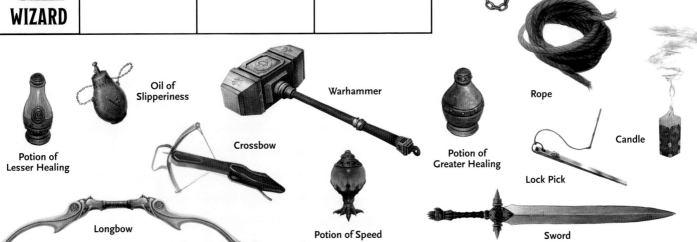

Grappling Iron

Rope

Candle

Oil of Slipperiness

Warhammer

Potion of Lesser Healing

Crossbow

Potion of Greater Healing

Lock Pick

Potion of Speed

Sword

Longbow

PAGE OF MANY THINGS

In a world filled with magic, there are sure to be a few wizards who like to experiment. The world of DUNGEONS & DRAGONS contains hundreds of strange and wonderful magic items, from the mundane to the reality-bending. Discover some of the weirdest, most powerful, and most iconic magic items in D&D lore.

STAFF OF THE MAGI

Any wizard worth their salt would love to wield this staff. As well as allowing the bearer to cast spells like *mage armour* at will, the staff contains 50 charges that can be used to cast powerful spells such as *fireball*, *summon monster*, and *plane shift*.

BAG OF HOLDING

A vital piece of equipment for any adventuring party, this magical bag is larger on the inside than it is on the outside. It can hold numerous heavy items, never weighing more than 15lbs to the bearer. However, if the bag is torn, its contents will be lost to the Astral Plane.

DECK OF MANY THINGS

Pick a card, any card ... but choose carefully. Drawing a card from the Deck of Many Things will have an instantaneous magical effect – some good, and some very, very bad.

BALANCE
Your alignment switches suddenly from good to evil, lawful to chaotic. Only neutral characters can avoid the mind-twisting power of Balance.

THE FATES
This powerful card allows whoever draws it to re-shape reality, erasing one event from the past entirely.

FLAMES
You gain a new, powerful enemy: a devil set on bringing about your destruction and ultimate death.

GEM
You're rich! Drawing this card immediately earns you a small fortune in jewellery and gems.

THE VOID
Drawing the Void means your soul is forced from your body and trapped in a phylactery ... and only the DM knows its whereabouts.

CARPET OF FLYING

Don't let the word order fool you – yes, it's a flying carpet. These items can carry up to 800 pounds at once, however, at a top speed of 4mph it may not be ideal if you're hoping to make a quick getaway.

ORBS OF DRAGONKIND

Bear one of these at your own risk. These orbs allow you to summon and control evil dragons – though you might not want to stick around if the orb is destroyed and the dragon is free of your thrall.

BAG OF BEANS

Similar to the Deck of Many Things, a Bag of Beans can produce a range of different magic effects, from summoning an angry treant to growing a small fruit tree.

IMMOVABLE ROD

Simple but effective, pressing the button on this rod will cause it to be fixed in one place and become almost impossible to move – be that blocking a door, attached to a wall, or even hanging in mid-air.

PORTABLE HOLE

With the appearance of a large sheet of black cloth, this will create a 10ft deep hole when unfolded and laid out on any solid surface. You could use this as a short-term prison or a way of smuggling secret items past guards.

RING OF WINTER

This ring grants the wearer many ice-based powers, including the ability to cast spells like *ice storm*, as well as preventing you from ageing when you wear it. However, it also contains a powerful chaotic magic that attempts to compel the wearer to harm those around them.

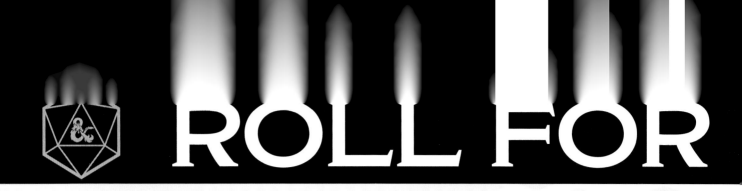
COMBAT 101

One of the things that all D&D players live to hear is 'roll initiative'. This signals the start of combat – but what happens after that? Read on to get the lowdown on how battling in Dungeons & Dragons really works.

ROLLING INITIATIVE

All combat starts with rolling initiative. Every player, plus monsters and NPCs, rolls a d20, adding their initiative bonus (Dexterity modifier). This determines the order of combat. The higher you roll, the sooner you'll get to attack! If two players roll the same number, the player with the highest Dex score gets to go first.

SURPRISE ROUNDS

If the encounter involves an ambush (either by the players or the enemies), the attackers may get a full round of combat before their opponents join in.

ACTIONS AND BONUS ACTIONS

There are three things you can do on a turn: Actions, Bonus Actions and Movement (up to your walking speed per round). Actions are usually weapon attacks or spells (and, in the case of certain classes, can be two or more attacks), but your DM may allow other things, too. Bonus Actions can be a few things: certain spells, giving Bardic Inspiration or taking a potion, for example.

FREE ACTIONS

Beyond your Action and Bonus Action, your DM may let you take a free action – this is usually something very simple, like talking to another player.

INSPIRATION

REACTIONS

Sometimes, you can react to another character's action on their turn. The most common Reaction is an Attack of Opportunity, which allows you to attempt to attack an enemy as they move out of melee range from you. The spell *hellish rebuke* is also a popular Reaction, allowing a mage to inflict fire damage on someone who has injured them.

MELEE AND RANGED FIGHTING

If you want to attack someone with a melee weapon, you will need to be within 5ft of them. Ranged weapons work better from a distance, and DMs will often impose disadvantage if you try to use them in close quarters.

HIT POINTS AND ARMOUR CLASS

When you do an attack, roll a d20 and add the weapon's attack bonus. If this number is equal to or greater than the target's armour class, it hits, at which point you can roll damage. When it's an enemy's turn, if their attack roll is higher than your AC, then they'll roll damage against you!

TIME FLIES...

As a general rule, a single round of combat is six seconds in-game. So if you're not sure if an Action is possible, ask yourself: could I do this in six seconds?

ADVANTAGE AND DISADVANTAGE

Sometimes, your DM may ask you to make a roll with Advantage or Disadvantage. If this happens, you will need to make two rolls; with Advantage, you take the higher of the two, while Disadvantage means you have to take the lower.

DEATH SAVES

If the worst happens and you drop to 0HP or below, it's not over yet! You get three Death Saving Throws. A d20 roll over 10 is a success, and under 10 is a failure. Three successful saving throws will stabilise you, but three failures will lead to death ... permanently. Luckily, if an ally is able to heal you before you reach that third failure, you should be fine!

WHERE IT BEGAN: FIRST EDITION

There are many editions of DUNGEONS & DRAGONS, each with their own mechanics, lore, and monsters. But where did it start? The first edition was created in 1974, and though it has changed massively since, you can still spot the pillars that support the game.

CHARACTERS

Classes

Far from the many character options of fifth edition, early D&D only had three character classes: cleric, magic-user (similar to fifth edition wizards) and fighting-man (similar to fighters).

Playable Peoples

The first playable peoples, then called 'races', were human, dwarf, elf, and hobbit (which was later changed to halfling).

MONSTERS & TREASURE

The game was originally released as a box-set that included a 40-page booklet called *Monsters & Treasure*, which featured the earliest D&D monsters, including orcs, purple worms, and, of course, dragons.

BASICS OF FIRST EDITION GAMEPLAY

Dice

Before the familiar seven-piece set, all you needed to play D&D were a handful of basic d6 dice. With a few exceptions, all attacks do 1d6 damage.

Hit points

A character's HP is determined by rolling hit dice – 1d6 per level. That means that, yes, if you're very unlucky, you could end up with a single hit point.

Character Death

First edition characters are very easy to kill. They start with few hit points, and can easily be permanently killed by a single hit in combat. Failed a saving throw against poison? I hope you have a backup character ready.

ORIGINAL SETTINGS

Before the Forgotten Realms (which weren't introduced to the world of D&D until over a decade later), there were Greyhawk and Blackmoor, the earliest DUNGEONS & DRAGONS settings. If you want to explore these classic worlds, the fifth edition adventure *Ghosts of Saltmarsh* is set in Greyhawk.

ADVANCED DUNGEONS & DRAGONS

A few years after D&D was first published, an updated version, called *Advanced Dungeons & Dragons* was released. This version is closer to the game we know today, adding numerous extra character options (including bards, paladins and thieves). This version contained the three core rulebooks: the *Player's Handbook*, *Monster Manual* and *Dungeon Master's Guide*.

PEOPLES OF

THINK BIG

When rolling a new character, it can never hurt to think big! With the inclusion of resources like *Volo's Guide to Monsters*, and *Xanathar's Guide to Everything*, there are dozens of options to choose from. If you want to stand head and shoulders above the rest, why not try some of these colossal folk?

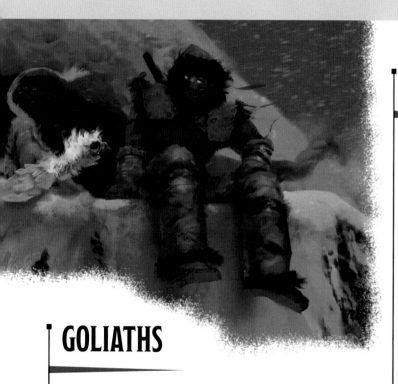

GOLIATHS

Towering over almost everyone else in the Forgotten Realms at up to eight feet tall, these enormous folk are easy to spot. Goliath tribes are commonly found high in the mountains, but they can be found across the Realms.

SPECIAL SKILLS:
A goliath's *stone's endurance* allows them to recover from injury faster and more easily.

KEY CLASSES:
Their natural Strength and Athletics ability make them excellent fighters and barbarians.

DID YOU KNOW?
Goliaths are easily recognisable by the tattoo-like dark patches on their skin, which they believe predict and guide their future.

FIRBOLGS

These gentle and reclusive folk are distantly related to giants – as evidenced by the fact they can grow to 10 feet tall! Their giant heritage makes them very strong, but their affinity with nature also allows them magical abilities.

SPECIAL SKILLS:
Firbolgs can communicate with plants and animals; though not well enough to hold full conversations, they can generally make themselves understood.

KEY CLASSES:
Their inherent Wisdom and connection to the wild make firbolgs excellent druids.

DID YOU KNOW?
Their massive size means that firbolgs have to eat twice as much as humans to survive.

THE REALM

WARFORGED

Native to the realm of Eberron, warforged are human-like constructs. Unlike other constructs, warforged have independent thought and their own ideas and beliefs.

SPECIAL SKILLS:
Their artificial nature means that warforged are a hardy folk who don't need to sleep or eat, and are immune to disease.

KEY CLASSES:
A versatile people, warforged can suit any class, from druid to paladin.

DID YOU KNOW?
Warforged don't bleed, but their artificial bodies do contain a blood-like fluid.

ORCS

Despite their aggressive reputation, orcs are as diverse as they are numerous. Found from the frozen tundra of Icewind Dale down to the tropical jungles of Chult, these hardy folk can make a home almost anywhere.

SPECIAL SKILLS:
A *primal intuition*, perhaps honed by a life in the wild, gives orcs extra proficiency in skills such as Animal Handling, Medicine, Nature, and Survival.

KEY CLASSES:
It may be tempting to make your orc a fighter or barbarian, but their knowledge of the wilderness can also make them fantastic clerics, rangers, and druids.

DID YOU KNOW?
Traditionally, orcs worship a one-eyed god called Gruumsh, though they come from all walks of life and beliefs.

GOBLINOIDS

GOBLINS
They may be popular monsters to throw at low-level parties, but goblins are also fun playable characters. Their *fury of the small* skill makes them potent against bigger creatures.

HOBGOBLINS
Bigger than goblins but smaller than bugbears, hobgoblins are often thought of as the brains of the goblinoid family – though this might not always be the case!

BUGBEARS
The biggest of the goblinoids, bugbears are very big – at up to eight feet – and very hairy! Despite their size, though, they're surprisingly stealthy and make fantastic rogues.

ROLL FOR

WHERE TO START?

As a Dungeon Master, the very beginning of your campaign can be one of the most daunting parts. There are so many unknowns. How are you going to introduce the player characters to the game? How will they all meet each other? And, most importantly, how are you going to set up their first quest? If you're struggling with where to start, here are a few suggestions.

AT A TAVERN

Taverns are great places to start a campaign because they're rife with possibility. It doesn't take a stretch of the imagination to come up with reasons for why the future party members are there, along with any number of useful non-player characters (NPCs). Once they're all in the same room, your options are endless.

Where Do You Go From There?
Wherever you like! Perhaps a fight breaks out and the party intervene, impressing a nearby merchant enough to hire them as bodyguards. Maybe they are approached by a mysterious stranger with a quest. Or they could overhear a conversation about a hidden treasure ...

IN PRISON

Starting in prison is a little different from the norm, but it can be helpful if you're a relatively new DM, or if you're worried about your party going off-piste too quickly. With a captive audience, you have the opportunity to introduce your world and set up your first plot hook without too many distractions. Plus, it gives players a chance to think about their character's backstory – how did they wind up in jail?

Where Do You Go From There?
The DM has a little more control over the next steps in this situation: the party could be offered a deal in exchange for their freedom, meet another inmate who knows about a job, or even stage a prison break!

INSPIRATION

EVE OF A BIG EVENT

The party have gathered in the town, city, kingdom, or wherever else on the eve of a big event. It's up to you as the Dungeon Master to decide what the event might be – it could be a fayre, with people from all over Faerûn attending to sell their wares, or some kind of tournament in which your party has an opportunity to compete.

Where Do You Go From There?

During an event, there are plenty of mini encounters you can set up – gladiatorial combat, games of chance ... any kind of competition, and each of these have different opportunities to reach different tangents in the story.

"I SUPPOSE YOU'RE WONDERING WHY I CALLED YOU ALL HERE ..."

If you want to steer your party into their first encounter, you can start the game under the assumption that they have already been approached or summoned by an NPC, ready to give them their first quest straight away. This can avoid any concerns you may have about how to present the first plot hook ... though, of course, the party can always choose to reject the offer and walk away.

Where Do You Go From There?

On the first adventure, of course! From there, you may get more quests from the same person, or find more places to explore along the way.

ON RAILS?

It's always tempting, particularly if you're new to DMing, to give your players a nudge in the direction you want them to go in. This is fine – though it's important to remember it's a collaborative game, so avoid too much railroading!

DESTINATION SEARCH

After travelling the length of the Forgotten Realms, legendary explorer Volo is settling down to write his next book. Can you find the locations he's visited in this wordsearch?

J	H	N	S	A	L	T	M	A	R	S	H	X	N	K	U	E	B	R	Y	V	C	H	B	Z	N	W
K	E	I	D	M	E	O	Y	H	M	P	O	R	T	N	Y	A	N	Z	A	R	U	D	A	B	S	Y
E	D	H	E	M	T	G	F	G	N	P	M	T	K	R	I	E	O	C	Y	V	T	L	R	P	E	R
C	E	B	E	M	A	K	I	N	E	O	R	U	Y	T	E	R	A	E	A	C	A	U	E	D	E	M
Z	E	E	W	A	S	R	E	E	A	A	T	N	U	J	E	W	R	T	B	J	M	S	N	Z	J	S
H	B	B	O	J	L	O	L	Y	R	E	R	D	E	R	V	C	G	P	V	U	R	K	U	D	F	G
I	S	A	E	P	R	S	D	N	O	R	U	E	D	M	I	T	H	R	A	L	H	A	L	L	R	A
S	C	G	X	G	Z	R	S	E	I	E	N	R	F	A	D	R	E	F	T	S	R	N	R	A	O	T
P	G	F	R	D	A	U	O	H	B	N	V	D	B	S	N	S	O	S	M	N	B	N	G	D	R	E
I	V	B	O	I	M	N	F	Y	C	R	D	A	X	P	U	I	E	Q	W	S	A	E	D	F	G	M
N	X	C	E	R	E	G	S	X	A	P	O	R	I	Y	A	W	N	I	N	G	P	O	R	T	A	L
E	S	X	V	N	T	U	L	E	L	O	K	K	Y	H	G	A	F	R	E	L	E	O	D	R	Y	N
O	F	C	H	U	L	T	A	I	E	U	R	Y	S	N	Z	T	A	G	S	H	A	V	A	A	A	T
F	E	G	D	A	E	R	U	E	Q	D	L	I	O	K	I	E	U	O	Y	E	M	F	N	C	J	R
T	Y	H	E	G	R	Y	G	T	R	V	K	F	L	G	T	R	S	J	E	E	D	D	F	K	A	T
H	W	H	P	A	R	I	H	M	I	C	E	W	I	N	D	D	A	L	E	M	S	Y	U	L	I	Z
E	I	T	I	T	O	E	T	V	H	B	C	G	F	G	R	E	D	C	M	L	O	K	O	E	D	G
W	L	U	B	H	E	B	E	H	U	F	D	S	Y	T	N	E	K	S	L	R	M	R	N	S	V	E
O	D	F	D	A	R	Y	R	T	G	R	Z	E	Z	W	R	P	V	E	F	Z	D	S	W	S	R	P
R	S	M	K	S	O	R	U	E	J	H	G	R	F	E	T	G	R	U	E	Z	V	G	D	S	B	H
L	A	K	U	G	U	I	Z	N	E	D	E	R	Z	E	U	B	E	J	R	K	G	O	Z	E	Z	A
D	N	A	B	R	V	R	F	T	R	A	E	S	W	O	R	D	C	O	A	S	T	K	W	A	M	N
I	G	S	E	O	E	U	R	O	A	B	G	E	G	V	E	H	G	J	A	I	E	W	G	U	S	D
G	X	S	P	V	O	S	U	W	B	G	D	Z	S	S	E	G	B	A	K	Z	I	G	Y	J	B	A
T	G	R	E	E	I	U	J	N	A	G	N	E	V	E	R	W	I	N	T	E	R	B	E	H	E	L
E	S	S	I	A	G	S	E	S	B	E	U	G	V	S	G	E	R	S	C	G	X	S	I	A	H	I
M	G	P	E	Y	E	I	G	R	G	B	A	L	D	U	R	S	G	A	T	E	S	O	S	R	G	N

YAWNING PORTAL
WATERDEEP
NEVERWINTER
ICEWIND DALE
TEN TOWNS
LUSKAN
FEYWILDS
UNDERDARK
SWORD COAST
BALDUR'S GATE
AGATHA'S GROVE
MITHRAL HALL
CHULT
PORT NYANZARU
WYRM'S GATE
SPINE OF THE WORLD
PHANDALIN
TRACKLESS SEA
FIELDS OF SLAUGHTER
SALTMARSH

DICE DISASTER

After a particularly hectic session, the party's dice have been knocked onto the floor. As they scramble to work out whose dice are whose, can you work out which set is incomplete? There should be seven dice in each set – a d4, d6, d8, d10, d12, d20 and d100.

TASHA'S CAULDRON OF EVERYTHING

Many players will know the spell *Tasha's hideous laughter*, which sends opponents into helpless giggles. But who is Tasha? Raised by the Mother of Witches, Baba Yaga, this legendary wizard dedicated her life to the discovery of new - often volatile - magic. Now, for the first time, her life's work has been published, featuring new class options, spells, artifacts, and much more.

CHARACTER OPTIONS

BARBARIAN
SUBCLASS: FORM OF THE BEAST

These truly wild barbarians transform into a bestial form when they enter a rage, attacking enemies with teeth, claws, and even spiked tails.

DRUID
SUBCLASS: CIRCLE OF SPORES

Druids who find beauty and hope in death and decay may be drawn towards the circle of spores, harnessing necrotic spores to attack enemies and even reanimate the dead.

WIZARD
SUBCLASS: BLADESLINGER

Not all wizards are bookish types – bladeslingers cast their magic through an elegant combination of swordplay and dance.

GROUP PATRONS

While warlocks have always garnered power from otherworldly patrons, *Tasha's Cauldron of Everything* offers the chance to have group patrons, who bind the whole party under their protection. Whether this is a sovereign, a criminal syndicate, or an ancient being, a patron will offer your party certain benefits in exchange for performing missions on their behalf.

MAGIC ITEMS

ATLAS OF ENDLESS HORIZONS

Mages who want to travel between planes may seek out the Atlas, which contains dimension-hopping spells including *arcane gate* and *plane shift*.

BABA YAGA'S MORTAR AND PESTLE

Created by Tasha's immortal adoptive mother, the properties of this item are nearly endless, ranging from brewing beer to travelling between realities.

TEETH OF DAHLVER-NAR

Carrying a pouch of teeth may be macabre, but the magical effects are worth it. Sowing a tooth in the ground will summon a magical creature to act on your behalf, while implanting them in your own mouth will give you great powers.

SPELLS

MIND SLIVER

Use this cantrip to shoot a spike of psychic energy directly into the mind of your enemies.

TASHA'S CAUSTIC BREW

One of Tasha's own spells, attack your enemies with a stream of magical acid.

SUMMON BEAST

This Level 2 spell allows Druids and Rangers to call a bestial spirit to their aid.

BLADE OF DISASTER

Attack your enemies with a blade-shaped planar rift using this Level 9 spell.

SIDEKICKS

A person or creature may choose to join your party as a companion. The *Cauldron of Everything* allows you to gain a sidekick of an equal level to the rest of the party, who can either be played by the DM or one of the players. These characters may help by providing expertise, assistance in combat or healing.

LIVE STREAMS

There's nothing more immersive than a game of D&D, which is why watching games has become insanely popular! Not only do you get to see the excitement, horror, and various other emotions on the players' faces, but you can also make sure that unbelievable roll of critical hits actually happened ...

HIGH ROLLERS

High Rollers has been running for over five years. "We sit down, play D&D and film it – and that's it," DM Mark Hulmes says. "There's no editing, we don't make things up for the camera, it's a genuine game of D&D."

AEROIS

Aerois is *High Rollers'* current campaign, which has been running for nearly three years. Set in a world created by Mark, it follows the heroes through all sorts of D&D hijinks and adventures.

Lucius Elenasto   Aila   Sentry

Nova V'Ger   Qillek Ad Khollar

LIGHTFALL

High Rollers' first campaign followed a party of adventurers in the land of Arrak, 46 years after a cataclysmic event called the Lightfall.

Jiŭtóu Zhìjī Jīng   Elora Galanodel

Reynard Ferehorn

Cam Buckland

Trellimar Aleath

GET INSPIRED

After playing D&D for over 15 years, Mark is full of advice for future Dungeon Masters. **"Just do it!"** he says. **"It's the scariest thing in the world, and people worry that they won't be good, but we were all like that when we started. You learn by doing. Don't worry about the rules. Don't look things up. Just go with your gut. As long as your friends are having fun, you did a good job."**

ACQUISITIONS INCORPORATED

This dark office comedy D&D spin-off has been going on since the days of 4th edition. It started out as a demo and playthrough of 4e, to show off what the game could do, and really took off when it became a live show at PAX, a series of gaming conventions between the US and Australia. Now, it sells out huge venues and has a huge following of loyal fans known as the Shadow Council.

THE LIVE SHOW

A few times a year – at nearly every PAX convention – *Acquisitions Incorporated* follows the staff of a fantasy franchise created to provide adventuring services for coin, and definitely not for any other, secret purposes.

Omin Dran, the half-elf cleric and CEO, is played by Jerry Holkins. Omin founded *Acq Inc* after taking out a loan from the Shadow Council to fund a quest to rescue his twin sister, Auspicia – who repaid him by starting her own franchise and attempting to acquire *Acq Inc*.

Every company needs a wizard, and *Acq Inc*'s wizard comes in the form of **Jim Darkmagic**, played by Mike Krahulik. Jim was the company's first employee, and has been reliably setting fire to things for many years.

Omin and Jim are joined by a whole cast of guest characters, including cheerful human paladin Evelyn Marthain (Anna Prosser), Viari the meta-gaming human bard (Patrick Rothfuss), Aeofel the acid-dissolved eladrin paladin (Wil Wheaton), tiefling "trash witch" sorcerer Strix Beestinger (Holly Conrad), Bobbie Zimmeruski the cheese-fuelled barbarian (WWE Superstar Xavier Woods) and terrifying elf ranger Môrgæn (Morgan Webb) – all under the watchful eye of DM Jeremy Crawford.

THE "C" TEAM

After a number of successful insider trades (some of which may have been with demonic entities), *Acq Inc* was able to diversify their portfolio into a weekly spin-off Twitch show, *The "C" Team*.

Walnut Dankgrass, played by Trystan Falcone, reps the natural world as the team's wood elf druid. Emerging from a mist shroud, **K'thriss Drow'b** is a drow warlock played by Kris Straub. Not your grandma's grandma, Kate Welch plays **Rosie Beestinger**, a halfling monk.

Donaar Blit'zen is a dragonborn narcissist (and paladin) played by Ryan Hartman.

The party are DMed by Omin Dran himself, Jerry Holkins, and are joined by special guest Anna Prosser as the ray of sunshine and tank, Evelyn Marthain.

START YOUR OWN FRANCHISE

The official *Acquisitions Incorporated* fifth edition sourcebook means that you, too, can start your own adventuring franchise. Producer Elyssa Grant says, **"we wanted to bring *Acq Inc* into the world in a way that allows new and veteran players alike to come in and enjoy it."** It introduces eight different job positions to choose from, including cartographer, secretarian and occultant, alongside a short campaign that lets you experience some of the staple moments from the original show, new spells, and stat blocks for iconic characters.

BEYOND THE

BALDUR'S GATE III

You awake aboard a Nautiloid ship with no memory of how you got there, only to discover you have been infected with a strange tadpole creature which, you believe, is slowly turning you into a mind flayer. In this incredible new video game, you and your companions must travel across worlds, facing strange cults, powerful foes, and difficult choices along the way.

GALE

After alighting from the wreckage of the Nautiloid ship, you come across Gale, a wizarding genius who claims to have been aboard the ship too. Gale is a master of magic – but will his drive for power and dangerous secret be his downfall?

WHAT IS A NAUTILOID?

These strange, shell-like flying ships are used by mind flayers to travel between worlds.

SHADOWHEART

This half-elf cleric is a loyal servant of a deity known as Shar, Mistress of the Night. When you first meet her, Shadowheart is on a mission on behalf of her dark mistress, but is struggling with unexplained outbursts of uncontrolled magic and a host of enemies on her tail.

TABLETOP

LAE'ZEL

Aboard the Nautiloid, you will meet a githyanki warrior who, like you, has been infected with a mind flayer parasite. Faced with turning into the very creature she has dedicated her life to destroying, she must purify herself before it is too late.

ASTARION

After being freed from the thrall of his sadistic master, this centuries-old vampire spawn is tasting freedom for the first time in his life. With the ability to walk in sunlight and resist his master's power, Astarion is now faced with a choice: become as cruel and powerful as his old master, or walk his own, lighter path.

WYLL

Meet the Blade of Frontiers, a legendary Baldurian hero ... who made a regrettable pact with a fiend in an attempt to atone for a deadly mistake he made in his past. Now, Wyll needs your help to track down his demonic patron and free himself from her control for good.

WELCOME TO AVERNUS

Part of your journey will take you through the infernal wastelands of Avernus, the first layer of the Nine Hells. Home to thousands of demons, devils, and their kin, Avernus seems to be a constant battleground between endlessly warring factions.

JUST GETTING STARTED

Of course, these are just a few of the folk you'll meet and places you'll visit. To discover the rest of the adventure, download the game now on PC and Google Stadia.

BOSS FIGHTS

As your party levels up, they will be able to take on stronger and more terrifying monsters in combat. After playing for months, sometimes even years, players may eventually find themselves face-to-face with some of the most powerful and iconic creatures in DUNGEONS & DRAGONS history.

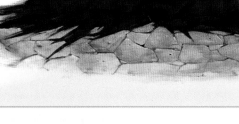

LICH

CHALLENGE RATING: 21

Mages who sacrifice their mortal soul in exchange for untold power will turn into liches. These undead creatures are highly intelligent and able to perform magic far beyond anything that a mortal could produce. They store their life essence in a magical artifact called a phylactery.

SKILLS

As well as being 19th level spellcasters, with the ability to cast spells ranging from *mage hand* all the way to the aptly-named *power word kill*, liches can also paralyse a creature with a single touch.

LEGENDARY ACTIONS

The ability *disrupt life* drains the life essence of any creature within 20 feet of the lich at the time of casting, while *frightening gaze* allows it to terrify anyone with a look.

HOW TO DEFEAT IT

In order to defeat a lich, you must first find and destroy its phylactery, otherwise it will be able to come back after being killed.

TARRASQUE

CHALLENGE RATING: 30

Not only is the tarrasque the most terrifying creature in the Forgotten Realms, it is also the highest-level monster in the DUNGEONS & DRAGONS bestiary. It sleeps for several years at a time but, when woken, its unquenchable hunger and drive for destruction means that it will attempt to very literally eat the entire world.

SKILLS

It can take five attacks on its turn, with its horns, spiked tail, razor-sharp claws, and enormous teeth. The tarrasque can also swallow creatures whole, and the unlucky victim will be subject to 16d6 acid damage at the beginning of each of the tarrasque's lengthy turns.

LEGENDARY ACTIONS

As well as taking an action on its own turn, the tarrasque can attack or move at the end of three other creatures' turns.

HOW TO DEFEAT IT

Besides being formidable in combat, the tarrasque is nigh-on impossible to kill, so your best chance is to trap it or send it back to sleep at the world's core.

KRAKEN

CHALLENGE RATING: 23

Adventurers taking to the seas should beware of the legendary kraken. Lurking in the depths of the ocean, krakens are enormous, squid-like monsters that prey on ships with their powerful tentacles, dragging unsuspecting sailors to their deaths.

SKILLS

Not only can a kraken attack creatures with its vicious teeth and tentacles, it can also create storms, calling down bolts of lightning to strike its enemies.

LEGENDARY ACTIONS

Krakens have the ability to expel clouds of pitch-dark ink, which plunge those nearby into darkness and cause poison damage to anyone unlucky enough to get caught in them.

HOW TO DEFEAT IT

They have immunity to most non-magical attacks, so your best chance against a kraken would be to attack with powerful magical weapons and spells.

PIT FIEND

CHALLENGE RATING: 20

The Nine Hells are filled with devils and demons, all with their own hierarchy of power. At the top of this hierarchy are pit fiends, vicious winged devils with not only an appetite, but a talent for inflicting pain and suffering on their victims.

SKILLS

Just being around a pit fiend can cause a powerful feeling of fear, making them hard to stand next to, never mind kill.

LEGENDARY ACTIONS

Perhaps the one positive to facing a pit fiend is that they don't have legendary actions – though they can make four attacks on a single action.

HOW TO DEFEAT IT

Whatever you do, don't attack them with fire. Pit fiends thrive in the fires of Hell and are immune to damage from it. Magical and silvered weapons should do the trick – if you can get close enough to use them.

PEOPLES OF

PLANE-TOUCHED

Beyond the Material Plane, where the Forgotten Realms reside, are many other planes – from the elemental to the celestial. Sometimes, beings are known to travel between the planes, and the Forgotten Realms are filled with fascinating people from many different worlds.

TRITONS

Hailing from the elemental plane of water, triton are, as you might imagine, an aquatic folk. They generally reside in the seas, building entire cities in the ocean's depths.

SPECIAL SKILLS:
Like water genasi, tritons are amphibious and can breathe underwater. Their connection to the water elemental plane also allows them to cast certain spells, like *wall of water*.

KEY CLASSES:
Strong and charismatic, triton suit many classes, and make particularly good paladins.

DID YOU KNOW?
Tritons have a strong affinity with animals and can communicate with many sea creatures, such as dolphins and giant seahorses.

GENASI

Touched by the elemental plane, these strange people are often the descendants of genies. From their unusual heritage, genasi gain traits and abilities based on one of the four elements – earth, fire, water, or air.

SPECIAL SKILLS:
The skills of a genasi depend on its elemental origin – for example, fire genasi are resistant to fire damage, while water elementals can breathe underwater.

KEY CLASSES:
Genasi are nothing if not versatile and can be well suited to a variety of classes. Their elemental affinity may lend itself to the sorcerer class.

DID YOU KNOW?
Earlier editions of D&D contained subclasses called para-genasi, representing elements including dust, ice, ooze, and smoke.

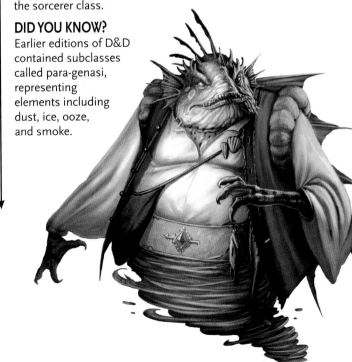

ELEMENTAL PLANE-TOUCHED
Sorcerers of draconic origin have certain elemental proficiencies in their casting styles. Why not try an elemental plane-touched Sorcerer, like a fire genasi?

THE REALM

AASIMAR

Originally descended from the union of humans and angels, aasimar bear the marks of being touched by the celestial plane. These angelic beings are often magically adept, and some retain the ability to sprout wings.

SPECIAL SKILLS:
Aasimar have powerful magics, including the ability to heal creatures with a touch.

KEY CLASSES:
Their charismatic nature means that aasimar make excellent spellcasters, such as sorcerers, paladins, and even bards.

DID YOU KNOW?
It is possible for aasimar to give birth to humans, and for the celestial trait to lie dormant for generations.

AARAKOCRA

As they soar through the air, you might easily mistake aarakocra for large birds. These bird-like humanoid people have beaks, wings, feathers, and talons – but also arms, legs, and an impressive ability with ranged weapons.

SPECIAL SKILLS:
As you might expect, aarakocra have the ability to fly on enormous, feathered wings, and feel at home in the air.

KEY CLASSES:
Aarakocra are very dextrous, which suits rogues, monks, and fighters well.

DID YOU KNOW?
Just as humans use facial expressions to show their mood, aarakocra sometimes pepper their speech with bird-like chirps which have different tones and meanings.

ANIMAL FOLK

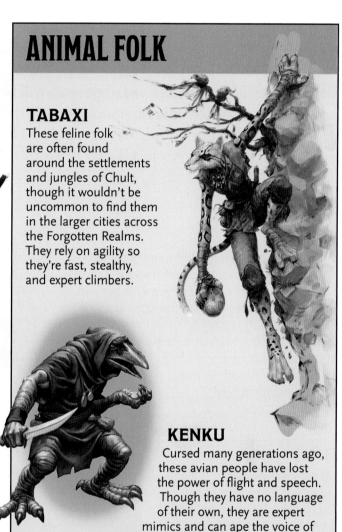

TABAXI
These feline folk are often found around the settlements and jungles of Chult, though it wouldn't be uncommon to find them in the larger cities across the Forgotten Realms. They rely on agility so they're fast, stealthy, and expert climbers.

KENKU
Cursed many generations ago, these avian people have lost the power of flight and speech. Though they have no language of their own, they are expert mimics and can ape the voice of almost anyone they hear.

TORTLES
Deep in the jungles of Chult live the tortles, a reptilian people with heavy, turtle-like shells on their backs. Though they can't swim well, they can hold their breath for well over an hour underwater.

MINSC (AND BOO)

Fans of the *Baldur's Gate* video games will be familiar with the enormous, soft-hearted (and perhaps soft-headed) ranger, Minsc, and his companion Boo. But who, exactly, are Minsc and Boo?

GROWING PAINS

Boo once took a potion of growth, which accidentally transformed him into a GIANT miniature giant space hamster! Very confusing indeed.

MINSC

Though he once dreamed of training at the prestigious Ice Dragon berserker lodge, Minsc instead found himself becoming a ranger and working as a bodyguard for the witch Dynaheir. Kind and fiercely driven by his desire to fight for good, Minsc's only goal in life is to destroy any evil he is faced with ... though he may sometimes need help determining who is and isn't evil.

BOO

Minsc's ever-loyal companion, the diminutive Boo is actually a miniature giant space hamster ... at least, that's what Minsc says. The ranger and hamster are a formidable team, and are rarely seen apart.

HUMBLE BEGINNINGS

Minsc was originally a player character in the home game of James Ohlen, the designer of the D&D video game *Baldur's Gate*.

ALLIES

DYNAHEIR

A powerful witch, Dynaheir was one of Minsc and Boo's first companions, as they served as her bodyguards. The duo travelled loyally by her side for years, until she was ultimately killed by an evil wizard.

THE BELOVED RANGER

For almost 80 years, a bronze statue of Minsc and Boo, called the Beloved Ranger, stood in the middle of Baldur's Gate to commemorate the heroic pair. Little did most people know, the statue was actually the real Minsc and Boo, petrified with magic. They weren't freed until a rogue spell by a wild mage broke the enchantment keeping them in statue form.

THE HEROES OF BALDUR'S GATE

Minsc and Boo travelled for several years with the adventuring party known as the Heroes of Baldur's Gate. The party included thief duo Krydle and Shandie, as well as a courageous cleric called Nerys, and Delina, the wild magic mage who ultimately freed Minsc and Boo from the petrification spell that trapped them for decades.

PERCEPTION CHECK

Success! The adventuring party has finally found their way through a particularly gruelling dungeon to the treasure that lies within. Can you test your perception skills by spotting the eight differences between these two scenes?

ASKING FOR DIRECTIONS

Disaster! While on a quest in the High Forest, the ranger's map has been sliced to shreds by an unexpected ogre attack. Can you put it back together, using the numbers provided?

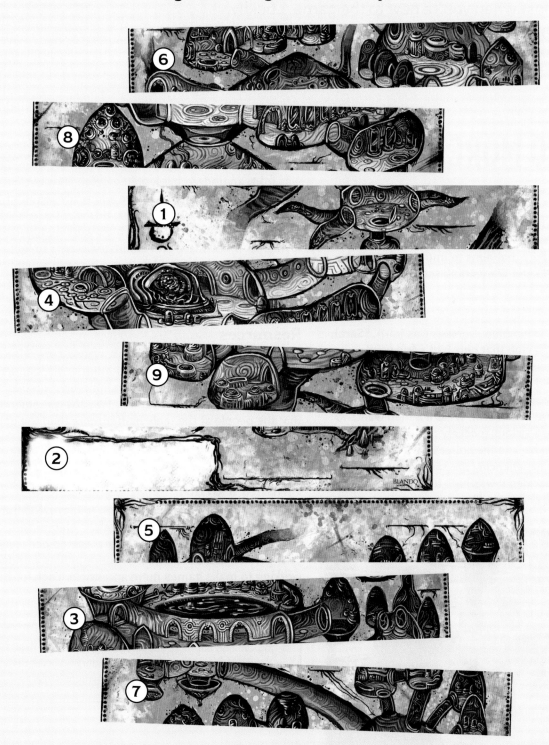

FIND YOUR PEOPLE

D&D boasts more players than any other RPG, with millions of fans worldwide. Still, with so many people, it can be easy to feel a little lost when you're new to the game. Luckily, there are people out there creating more and more spaces for players from all walks of life, making the D&D world more inclusive and fun than ever.

NO MORE DAMSELS

Have you ever looked around an RPG night and thought, "Wow, there's not a lot of people like me in here"? Sarah Pipkin and Naomi Clarke have, which is why they created *No More Damsels*, a London-based charity that aims to improve the gender balance of the RPG and Wargaming scene.

Origin Story

Naomi tells us how *No More Damsels* was born. **"Sarah and I were part of a club that only had a few women in it. We wanted to celebrate those players and encourage a more diverse crowd to join the club. Unfortunately, when we suggested a 'women-only DM' event, the club founder looked us in the eye and asked, 'What if a man wants to DM, though?', like a vicious mockery cantrip straight to the heart. We went back to the notice board and found a lot of people were experiencing the same issues and felt unheard. So, we decided it was high time that we stopped being seen as side characters!"**

Events

NMD launched in 2019 with an event where every DM was from an underrepresented gender. **"It was clear we'd discovered something inclusive and really beautiful,"** Naomi says. **"For lots of players, this was their first time seeing a collective of DMs like ours working together and loving it!"** Since then, they've hosted events to help lower the barrier of entry to tabletop gaming: game nights, workshops and panels where they highlight the work of women, trans and nonbinary people.

Resources

Beyond events, *No More Damsels'* website provides resources for those who want to improve the gender balance of their games, making sure every experience at the table is as good as it can be. **"We always remember that the people at the table matter more than the game itself,"** Naomi says. **"If one of us isn't having fun, the game isn't working."**

Finding a Group

"The best thing to do is say, 'I want to play D&D but I've never played before. Please help!'" Naomi says. **"If you're worried about not being accepted because of your gender, there are a host of communities worldwide working to make games more accessible. Look for them."**

You can find out more about *No More Damsels* at their website (nomoredamselsrpg.org), Twitter and Instagram @NMDLondon, and Facebook @nomoredamsels.

Images Copyright © 2021 Naomi Clake

THREE BLACK HALFLINGS

Image credit needed

Who Are The Three Black Halflings?

Luyanda Unati Lewis-Nyawo, Jeremy Cobb and Jasper William Cartwright make up *Three Black Halflings*, a thoughtful and hilarious podcast all about diversity in D&D. They share tips for DMs and players, talk about some of the ways to approach different cultures in your game, and approach the issue of diversity with as much respect as possible. And they laugh a lot.

Thinking about Things Differently

Three Black Halflings is all about creating inclusive, accessible spaces in the world of D&D. **"It's great to watch how not only people of colour but allies can find a space where they feel like they're being armed with the necessary tools to make their tables more diverse without feeling like it's a hot potato realm that you can't touch,"** Unati says, adding, **"Come, it's nice here! We have sun!"**

The Cub and the Caterpillar

Jeremy, Jasper and Unati's actual-play series, The Cub and the Caterpillar, follows the many hijinks of Ongenagama, a golden axe-wielding Lionblood fighter, and Mooti, a Daa'ima (moth-person) sorcerer/bard. Dropped into the world of Wagadu, the heroes can't

remember what their lives were like before they arrived there, and are left to make their way through a chaotic world of gods, spirits and ancestors.

THE WAGADU CHRONICLES

Created by Allan Cudicio, the Wagadu Chronicles is an African-inspired campaign setting that asks: What would high fantasy be like if J.R.R. Tolkien had been born in Africa? "It's interesting because of its focus on lineages rather than races or species," Unati says. "The freshness of the Africa-based world was really exciting, too."

Creating a Community

Though *Three Black Halflings* is a relatively new podcast, they've already created a thriving community of D&D lovers. Jasper says, **"From very early on, we started receiving messages from people saying how much they connected with the show. I think people really enjoyed the fact that they could go somewhere and talk about these difficult things, but not in a doom-and-gloom way. It's still fun and accessible."** The community is very active on Discord, providing support, new ideas ... and hundreds of memes!

Where to Start?

What's their advice for new D&D players who don't know where to start? **"Don't be scared!"** Unati says, and Jeremy adds, **"It's a lot of fun! There are a lot of rules, but just jump in and figure it out as you go. The point is to have fun and tell a story with your friends. Even if you don't have friends with you, you can go on sites like Roll20. On our Discord, people have set up online games, even with people they don't know."**

Three Black Halflings are a member of the Headgum podcast network. You can also listen to them on Spotify, Apple Podcasts and Google Podcasts, and find them on Twitter @TBHalflings.

ACROSS FAERÛN

NEVERWINTER WOOD

Located on the Sword Coast, Neverwinter Wood is a hub of magic, with many communities of elves and other fae living within it. From the beautiful city of Neverwinter itself, through to the dark and mysterious caves of The Crags mountain range, these woods hold something for any explorer on the hunt for a new adventure.

TOWER OF TWILIGHT

This magical tower, located on an island within a small lake, is only visible to the naked eye in starlight. If you're lucky enough to see it, you can marvel at its stunning, twisted, emerald-green towers ... and perhaps even pay a visit to the wizard who lives within.

NEVERWINTER RIVER

The Neverwinter region gets its name from this river, whose waters run warm all year round, giving the city a pleasantly moderate climate, even in winter. Many believe that the waters get their warmth from the fire elementals that live on the nearby Mount Hotenow.

THE CRAGS

This mountain range contains the volcano, Mount Hotenow, from which a river of pure elemental fire flows. The fact that it plays home to many fire elementals, as well as fire giants and red dragons, makes it dangerous terrain for even the most courageous adventurers.

The Crags

Mount Hotenow

Neverwinter Wo

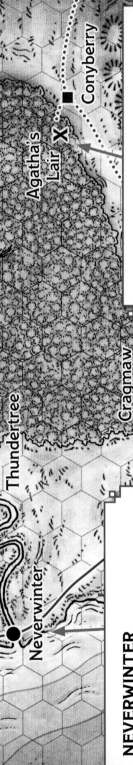

Conyberry

Agatha's
Lair **X**

Cragmaw
Castle

Thundertree

Neverwinter

AGATHA'S GROVE

Deep in the forest, well-hidden from prying eyes, lies the lair of the banshee Agatha, who jealously guards her home and the treasures within. As well as possessing magical knowledge, Agatha has a deadly wail that can kill those who hear it.

NEVERWINTER

Welcome to the Jewel of the North! With its grand buildings and pleasant year-round climate, the bustling city of Neverwinter is a popular spot for people from all walks of life. It is particularly well-known for the beautiful gardens which are cultivated all over the city.

CREATURES OF NEVERWINTER WOOD

TREANT

Treants are large, sentient, often ancient trees. Mostly peaceful creatures, they sometimes surround themselves with poisonous violet fungi in order to ward off attackers.

ETTERCAP

Arachnophobes beware! These six-foot-tall spider-like creatures that lurk in Neverwinter Wood have sharp claws and a venomous bite. Fond of other arachnids, they often come accompanied by one or more giant spiders.

AWAKENED SHRUB

Small, bush-like plants animated using magic, these little guys can often be found as helpers or familiars to wizards and druids. They're not a huge threat but why would you want to attack them?

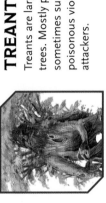

BANSHEE

Sometimes called 'groaning spirits', banshees are malevolent spectres, who fight off trespassers with their piercing, murderous wail. They can be found all across the wood, but most famously in Agatha's Grove.

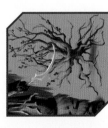

ROLL FOR

LEARN FROM THE (DUNGEON) MASTERS

No game of D&D is possible without a Dungeon Master to run the story, play the NPCs, control monsters and create a whole world for the players to explore. Running your first game can be daunting, but luckily, some of D&D's best Dungeon Masters have provided some top tips to get you started.

PLAY YOUR OWN GAME

The Adventure Zone's Travis McElroy reminds us not to get too wrapped up in what other people are doing: **"It's important to see how other people do it and to learn what you can, but at the end of the day, you have to play your own game."**

GO WITH YOUR GUT

With three core source books, plus dozens of other official modules and books, it's easy to get stressed out by the rules, but *High Rollers*' Mark Hulmes is here to reassure you. **"Don't worry about the rules. Don't look things up in the moment. Just go with your gut and look it up later. You don't want to feel like everything has to be about the rules."**

LEAD BY EXAMPLE

The DM has a big role to play in setting the tone of any game, says *How We Roll*'s Joe Trier. **"A good tool is to lead by example. If you want a role-play focused campaign, try starting with an NPC talking to them in first person. The DM sets the style, so encourage your players and don't be afraid to make a fool of yourself. Show, don't tell."**

INSPIRATION

LEARN TO RELAX

DMing for the first time might be scary, but *Acquisitions Incorporated*'s Jerry Holkins is here to reassure you. **"The most important thing to remember when you're behind that screen is that the players don't know what you have planned,"** he says. **"Any nervousness you have about how things are gonna go is just wasted energy. As far as they know, that thing you came up with off the top of your head was the plan from the beginning. Learning to relax, and to be okay with the natural ebb and flow of your table, is the best skill you can develop. This is a skill you'll need for the rest of your life, and not just at the table: to make peace with the moment."**

Images Copyright © 2021 Penny Arcade

Images Copyright © 2021 Critical Role Productions LLC

FIND YOUR VOICE

Critical Role's Matt Mercer has some great advice for DMs who are a little nervous about voicing NPCs. **"The truth is, while voices are helpful, they are far from necessary. Even just clear physicality can radically change how a character is presented and remembered. Hunched forward with a furrowed brow reads very differently than a confident stance with shoulders back. A raised nose and crossed arms will be distinct against a nervous scratcher who is always looking over their shoulder. Noting the general way an NPC holds themselves is a fun, clear way to define them both for yourself and your players."**

KEEP IT SAFE

Player safety is vital, as *Three Black Halflings*' Jasper Cartwright tells us. **"If you're nervous, just establish safety rules. If there are any subjects you'd rather not talk about, that make you uncomfortable, get that out in the open early on. Then you're free to enjoy the game without worrying about that upsetting the flow. Just embrace the chaos of the dice!"**

Images Copyright © 2021 Three Black Halflings

ODDITIES

The world of DUNGEONS & DRAGONS is rife with fascinating creatures, from the commonplace to the very, very odd. If your party thinks they've seen it all, why not try introducing some of these baffling beasts to your campaign to really shake things up?

GELATINOUS CUBE
CHALLENGE RATING: 2

No campaign is really complete without a gelatinous cube encounter. Just as you might expect, this is a large, slow-moving cube made of a jelly-like substance. Though it might not look like much, those who are caught in a gelatinous cube's mass will be paralysed and dissolved by the cube's acidic digestive juices, leaving only their bones and weapons suspended within the ooze.

MYCONID
CHALLENGE RATING: 1

Not all creatures who lurk in the Underdark are vicious predators. These mushroom-like humanoids favour shadowy caverns and dark tunnels simply because they like the peace and quiet. They avoid violence whenever possible and may even offer help and shelter to adventurers who respect their peaceful nature.

GIBBERING MOUTHER
CHALLENGE RATING: 2

Created by strange, dark magic, the gibbering cry of these bafflingly-named monsters confounds those that hear it, allowing the mouther to attack ... with six fang-filled mouths at once. Every creature that a gibbering mouther consumes is absorbed into its body, adding more eyes and another mouth to its hideous mass.

YOCHLOL
CHALLENGE RATING: 10

Be wary of that pretty elven woman who's new to town – yochlol are shapeshifting demons who, in their natural form, resemble writhing pillars of bright yellow ooze. They can also take the form of beautiful women or giant spiders, and can read the minds of unwary passers-by at will.

GRELL
CHALLENGE RATING: 3

Originally from the Far Realm, an outer plane of madness, grell are bizarre abberations that resemble floating, tentacled brains with beaks. Though they have no eyes, they have excellent hearing and a strange, electrical blindsense that allows them to track down victims even in the pitch black.

FLUMPH
CHALLENGE RATING: 1/8

Flumphs are gentle, benevolent, and often highly intelligent creatures. Though they feed off the mental energy of other creatures, they only take what they need and very rarely hurt those they feed off. The colour of a flumph changes depending on its mood, turning bright red if it is exposed to evil or unpleasant thoughts, blue if it's sad, and pink if it's happy.

MODRON
CHALLENGE RATING: 1/8

Another outer-planar species, modrons are immortal constructs that represent order and neutrality. They take on various different geometric shapes, and you can generally tell how high-ranking a modron is by how many sides it has, with some even appearing as humanoid.

CATOBLEPAS
CHALLENGE RATING: 5

Is it a camel? Is it a buffalo? Is it a dinosaur? Whatever it is, it's utterly bizarre. Catoblepas lurk in swamps, hunt during the full moon, and omit such a foul stench that adventurers may risk being poisoned if they get too close!

VECNA

Over his many centuries of life, wizard-turned-lich-turned-god, Vecna, has gone by many different monikers. If you hear of the Lord of the Rotted Tower, the Chained God or Master of the Spider Throne, you might be about to come face-to-face with one of DUNGEONS & DRAGONS' greatest villains.

BACKGROUND

Even in life, Vecna was a feared wizard. Mastering dark magic, he built an empire through violent and sinister means, in time gaining enough power to complete the lich ritual. After several centuries of mortality, Vecna was betrayed and murdered by a lieutenant, the vampire Kas. Though his body was destroyed, Vecna's spirit grew in power, ultimately reaching godhood.

ARTIFACTS

When his physical form perished, Vecna left behind a few parts that held great power, which adventurers may happen upon on their travels.

THE HAND OF VECNA

One of the only pieces of Vecna's body that remained after his bloody battle with Kas, the Hand of Vecna can fuse with its bearer and grant them incredible abilities. But beware — as with many powerful magic items, the power of the Hand can also corrupt.

THE EYE OF VECNA

Replacing one of your own eyes with Vecna's disembodied one will grant the bearer, among other things, x-ray vision, an immunity to poison and disease, and the opportunity to wield the hugely-powerful *wish* spell.

THE SWORD OF KAS

Once a gift from Vecna to his loyal lieutenant, Kas ultimately turned the sword on his master, destroying his physical body. Wielding the sword will allow you to channel the spirit of Kas — though it will constantly attempt to overpower you, demanding that it be bathed in blood.

ENEMIES

KAS

Once Vecna's most trusted right-hand man, Kas was eventually corrupted by a powerful magical sword, which convinced him to turn on his master. In the battle, Vecna's body was destroyed, leaving behind only his left hand and an eye, while Kas was imprisoned in the Plane of Ash, eventually turning into a vampire known as Kas the Bloody-Handed.

THE LADY OF PAIN

Following one of Vecna's grabs for power, which involved an attempted invasion of the multi-dimensional city of Sigil, the City of Secrets, he made a powerful enemy of Sigil's enigmatic ruler, the Lady of Pain.

THE RAVEN QUEEN

The Raven Queen is a powerful deity who rules over the dominions of life and death. Jealous of her ability to harvest souls, Vecna repeatedly tried to invade her fortress in the Shadowfell and overthrow her, making the two beings immortal enemies.

SIREN'S CALL

While on a voyage, you and your party have fallen victim to the lure of a siren. Your only way of escape is to answer her riddles, or else perish in her lair.

1 The poor have me. The rich need me. If you eat me, you will certainly die. What am I?

_____

2 Smile at me and I'll smile back, but if you drop me, I will crack. What am I?

_____

3 The paladin rode into Waterdeep on Friday. He stayed for three days, then left on Friday. How is this possible?

_____

4 I have a mouth but cannot speak. I always run but never walk. What am I?

_____

5 I contain towns without houses, forest without trees, mountains without boulders and waterless seas. What am I?

_____

6 What can be found at the beginning of everything and the end of time and space? It is the beginning of the end and the end of before.

_____

7 What is passed from father to son, and shared between brothers? It belongs to you, but is used more by others.

_____

A FISHY SITUATION

A suspicious-looking gnome in a tavern has bet you ten silver that you can't solve his "unsolvable" matchstick puzzles. Do you feel confident enough to take his bet?

Can you flip the fish around by moving only three matches? No match should overlap.

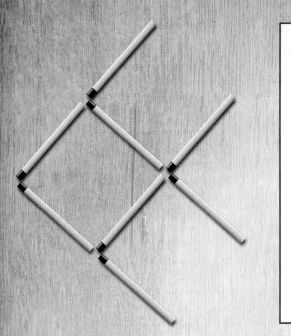

Can you turn the donkey around by moving just one match?

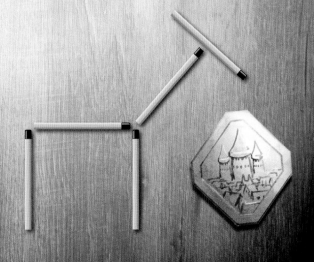

CREATING NPCs

So you're planning a new campaign. You've set up your world, planned the encounters, and rolled up the player characters ... what now? Well, you're going to need to fill your world with NPCs (non-player characters) for your players to interact with. From tavern-keepers to end-game bad guys, let's start with a few pointers on NPC creation.

BACKGROUND CHARACTERS

Before you start bringing in beloved allies and big bads, your players will need people to sell them items, serve them drinks, give them information, and to generally interact with. It's a good idea to keep a few 'generic' NPCs in your back pocket that could crop up anywhere, in case the players go in a direction you weren't expecting!

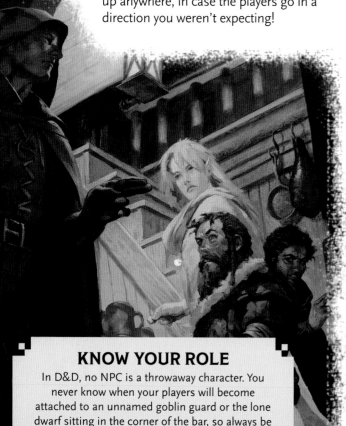

QUEST-GIVERS

Mysterious strangers in taverns, wealthy merchants, local lawmakers ... quest hooks can come from almost any well-placed NPC. When you're creating these NPCs, think about how your players will react to them. You need to motivate them to take the quest on offer, whether that's through money, threats, or gentle persuasion ... and the character has to be intriguing enough that the players don't just walk away!

KNOW YOUR ROLE

In D&D, no NPC is a throwaway character. You never know when your players will become attached to an unnamed goblin guard or the lone dwarf sitting in the corner of the bar, so always be prepared to improvise!

VOCAL TALENT

You may feel self-conscious when you first start role-playing, but coming up with voices for different NPCs can make them more convincing and help immerse your players in the world of the game.

INSPIRATION

ALLIES

Often, parties will join up with allies who may help them in adventures, whether they're joining them on quests or providing information. These NPCs sometimes start as background characters, who get 'promoted' when players like them. These players can be useful DM tools, giving players relevant information or nudging the party in the right direction if they start to stray too wildly off-piste.

WHAT'S IN A NAME?
Naming NPCs on the fly can be surprisingly difficult, so keep a list of potential character names to hand in case you need one.

ENEMIES

What is an adventuring party without a foe to defeat? From campaign-spanning villains to easy-to-defeat henchmen, creating enemy NPCs is one of the most fun parts of DMing a game. Think about your villain's motivations. In a long-running campaign, it can get boring if every single villain wants to kill for the sake of killing, so try giving them different personalities and goals. Plus, making complex antagonists can present your players with interesting moral quandries beyond simply defeating them in combat.

BE PREPARED
You never know when you will need to throw an NPC into combat, so it's helpful to have stat blocks even for minor characters. *The Monster Manual* has pre-rolled stat blocks for many different characters of varying levels.

IT SPELLS TROUBLE

There are many different types of caster, from sorcerers, who are born with their power flowing through their veins, and wizards, who study for years to hone their craft, to bards, who channel enchantments through their music. With hundreds of varied spells available, let's explore some of the most iconic ones to add to your magical arsenal.

ELDRITCH BLAST

LEVEL: Cantrip
CLASS: Warlock

With 1d10 damage, this is one of the most powerful cantrips in D&D. As warlocks level up, they gain extra beams to their *eldritch blast,* allowing them to attack more than one target at once – or to really lay into one!

MAGIC MISSILE

LEVEL: 1
CLASS: Sorcerer, wizard

Having been around since the first edition of D&D, *magic missile* is a fan-favourite, and a must-have spell for any magic user. The caster shoots three bolts of energy at their enemies – and, most importantly, doesn't even require an attack roll to hit.

(MELF'S) ACID ARROW

LEVEL: Cantrip
CLASS: Wizard

Named after the creator of the spell, an elf mage who played with D&D creator Gary Gygax's in his home game, this magical arrow continues to inflict acid damage after it successfully hits, doing further damage on the target's subsequent turns in combat.

SAVE THE DAY
Some spells require a Saving Throw from the target in order to take an effect. Saving Throws are made against the caster's Spell Save DC (Difficulty Class), which is usually equal to 8 + proficiency bonus + the caster's spellcasting skill modifier.

CHARM PERSON

LEVEL: Cantrip
CLASS: Bard, druid, sorcerer, warlock, wizard

Popular with bards, *charm person* lets you convince a target that you are a good friend for up to an hour, which can prove invaluable in countless situations, from avoiding a deadly conflict to persuading a tavern owner to give you a good rate on a room ... or your drinks.

FIREBALL

LEVEL: 3
CLASS: Sorcerer, wizard

There aren't many sorcerers who don't revel in casting a *fireball* or two. Even on a successful saving throw, this wonderfully flamboyant spell does a minimum of 4d6 fire damage – though its 20ft radius can risk the flames hitting allies and bystanders.

EVARD'S BLACK TENTACLES

LEVEL: Cantrip
CLASS: Wizard, warlock, fighter (eldritch knight)

One of the most visually dramatic spells, this spell – as you might imagine – causes black, eldritch tentacles to sprout on the ground, bludgeoning anyone within range and restraining those who try to cross them.

POLYMORPH

LEVEL: 4
CLASS: Bard, druid, sorcerer, wizard

This marvellously versatile spell allows the caster to turn a creature – be that an ally, enemy, or the caster themselves – into an animal.

POWER WORD KILL

LEVEL: 9
CLASS: Bard, sorcerer, warlock, wizard

One of the deadliest spells in a mage's arsenal, *power word kill* has the ability to cause instant death. A word, chosen by the caster to be infused with deadly enchantment, is spoken, and any target with under 100 hit points dies immediately.

WISH

LEVEL: 9
CLASS: Sorcerer, wizard

There are few spells more powerful than *wish*, which can re-shape the fabric of reality itself at the request of its user. The possibilities are both vague and broad, and the extent of what *wish* can do is up to the DM. Be careful, though, as the effort of casting this spell can damage the caster!

XANATHAR

Far below Waterdeep lies the subterranean city of Skullport, a shadowy port where you may run into the infamous elder beholder crime lord, Xanathar.

BACKGROUND

Many different beholders have held the title of Xanathar over the years. The most famous, originally known as The Eye, had the original Xanathar assassinated and took over its name and position at the head of the Xanathar Thieves' Guild. After The Eye's eventual death at the hands of a powerful lich, several others took up the mantle and carried on its notorious legacy.

ORGANISATIONS

Agents of the Eye
This was the first criminal gang formed by The Eye, before it took on the title of Xanathar. Originally a slaving ring, it was eventually merged with the Xanathar Thieves' Guild to form one powerful criminal organisation.

Xanathar Thieves' Guild
In order to join the ruthless Thieves' Guild, members had to prove their loyalty by committing a violent crime against a family member or close friend. Though the guild has a few hundred members, the identity of Xanathar is a closely guarded secret, known to only a few loyal guild members.

WHAT IS A BEHOLDER?

Beholders are underground creatures that appear as giant, floating eyeballs, with several more eyeballs on the end of eyestalks. They are powerful magical creatures, known for their cunning, and are notoriously difficult to sneak up on.

RIVALS

Unyielding Sword
This mercenary company fell under the ruthless eye of Xanathar when they unknowingly kidnapped one of his agents to sell into slavery.

Iron Ring
Along with the Shadow Thieves, this crime ring is one of the only major rivals to the Xanathar Thieves' Guild. Their members are easily identified by the iron keyrings they wear on their belts.

Misker the Pirate Tyrant
Another beholder, Misker is a smuggler and one of Xanathar's greatest professional rivals. He wears eyepatches over two of his eyestalks, which were rumoured to have mysterious, legendary powers.

XANATHAR'S GUIDE TO EVERYTHING

In its time as Skullport's most notorious crime lord, Xanathar has gathered a wealth of valuable information. This official book contains new rules for different class options, spells, encounters, tools and magic items.

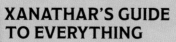

LOST IN THE CROWD

Your party has been tasked with tracking down a goblin artificer called Fezzik at a party but he's disguised himself among some of his brethren. Can you spot the one that looks slightly different? That's Fezzik!

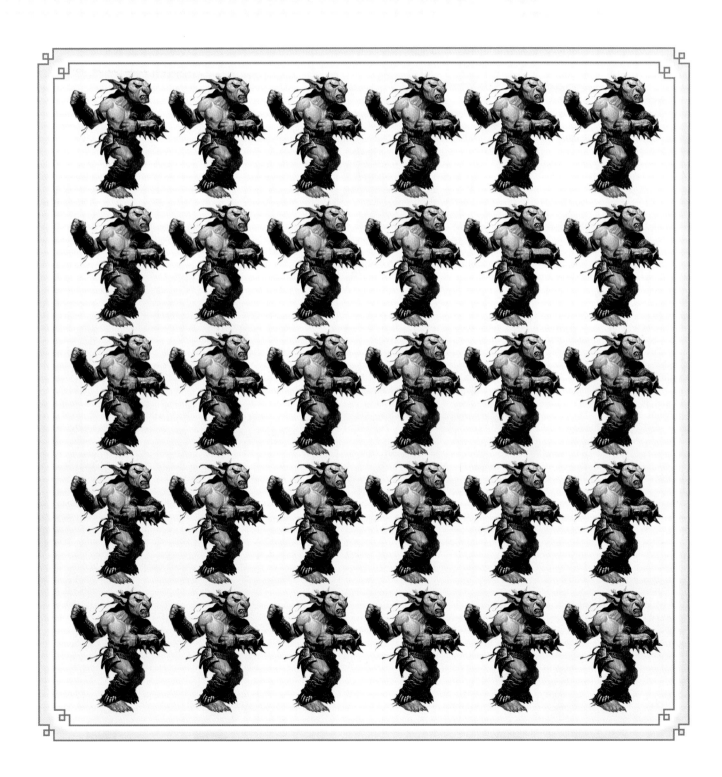

 ANSWERS ON PAGES 92-93

X MARKS THE SPOT

A mysterious patron has given your party a map that supposedly leads to a legendary treasure. Follow the directions found below to discover the location where the loot is hidden. Begin your journey from square 2F.

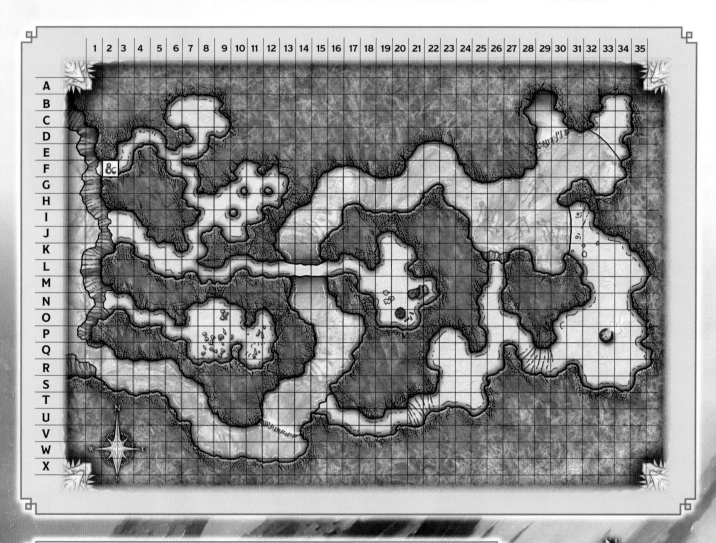

East 5, South 2, East 1, South 4, East 6, South 2, East 1, South 6, East 8, North 3, East 10, North 6, West 4, North 5, East 4, North 3

CAMPAIGN

DESCENT INTO AVERNUS

In the midst of a demonic war, the holy city of Elturel has mysteriously descended into Avernus, the first of the Nine Hells. This campaign takes your party from Baldur's Gate into the depths of the infernal plane, piloting demonic war machines and battling powerful devils in an attempt to restore Elturel to its rightful place in the Forgotten Realms.

WHERE TO START?

Players will start in the (non-infernal) city of Baldur's Gate, where they can take on a few smaller, sandbox-style quests to help them level up before they face the Nine Hells. The book offers a starter quest, in which the party is employed by a mercenary company, the Flaming Fist, to investigate a group of sinister cultists.

MAKING DEALS WITH DEVILS

When you're in Hell, you can't just fight everything you meet – or your party may not last very long. Luckily, the campaign offers opportunities to make deals with the devils you meet, forming tentative alliances in order to restore Elturel and, perhaps, escape the Nine Hells once and for all.

SPOTLIGHT

BE CAREFUL WHO YOU TALK TO

Moreso than other campaigns, the outcome of *Descent into Avernus* relies on choices that players make early in the game. Be careful – the way you interact with a seemingly nondescript NPC in a low-level encounter may come back to bite you in a few sessions!

DARK SECRETS

From the beginning of the campaign, the party will be bound by a shared sinister secret, chosen by the players and DM during character creation. Perhaps they were involved in a failed political coup, or were witnesses to a bloody murder

INFERNAL WAR MACHINES

One of the most popular features of the campaign, *Descent into Avernus* introduces mechanics for piloting and battling massive infernal war machines. They're powered by damned souls and have their own defence and health stats too. But treat them gently as they're prone to mishaps – an element of the game that can cause them to flip over, slow down, or even explode.

LOCATIONS

BALDUR'S GATE

Since the disappearance of Elturel, the port city of Baldur's Gate has been overrun with refugees from the missing city and is plagued with demons, cultists, and numerous other infernal horrors for your party to take on.

AVERNUS

Few adventuring parties are willing to face the misery of the Nine Hells, the Forgotten Realms' infernal plane. The campaign allows you to explore Avernus, the first layer of Hell, in brilliant, dark detail.

CLASSIC CAMPAIGNS

With over 40 years of history, DUNGEONS & DRAGONS has an enormous amount of unique adventures from over the years to choose from. Many of the classic campaigns from older editions in the early days of AD&D have been "translated" into fifth edition rules in recent years, so you can dig into some classic games of yore ...

TOMB OF HORRORS

ORIGINAL SYSTEM: First edition
FIND IT IN: *Tales from the Yawning Portal*

True to its name, Tomb of Horrors was first designed by D&D creator Gary Gygax all the way back in the early 1970s ... and it's a killer. The vicious dungeon, leading to the lair of legendary lich Acererak, is littered with traps, many of which can instantly kill an unsuspecting adventurer. Only the bravest of high-level characters should attempt this module ... and be sure to have a few extra character sheets handy.

RAVENLOFT

ORIGINAL SYSTEM: First edition
FIND IT IN: *Curse of Strahd Revamped*

Lurking within a pocket dimension of the Prime Material Plane lies Ravenloft, otherwise known as the Demiplane of Dread. As you may expect, Ravenloft is a sinister place, surrounded by deadly fog and rife with dark magic. Those brave enough to venture there may find themselves in the crosshairs of the powerful vampire wizard who rules over the realm, Strahd von Zarovich. The original Ravenloft module has been adapted for fifth edition as Curse of Strahd Revamped, allowing new adventurers to explore the darkest corners of the demiplane.

THE SINISTER SECRET OF SALTMARSH

ORIGINAL SYSTEM: First edition
FIND IT IN: *Ghosts of Saltmarsh*

Adventurers in the early campaign setting of Greyhawk may find themselves in the seaside town of Saltmarsh. First published in the early 1980s, The Sinister Secret of Saltmarsh contains everything you could want in a module – haunted houses, on-ship battles, and a whole cast of curious characters to encounter.

THE FORGE OF FURY

ORIGINAL SYSTEM: Third edition
FIND IT IN: *Tales from the Yawning Portal*

Designed for level 3-5 characters, Forge of Fury may be an ideal following-on point from The Sunless Citadel. Players can explore the caverns of an abandoned dwarven stronghold, battling brutal monsters, and discovering the treasures in an ancient hoard, guarded by a mysterious dragon.

ISLE OF THE ABBEY

ORIGINAL SYSTEM: Second edition
FIND IT IN: *Ghosts of Saltmarsh*

Hired by the local mariner's guild to investigate the aftermath of a bloody battle between sinister clerics and vicious pirates on the seemingly abandoned Abbey Isle, your party will have the chance to take on undead, living constructs, and brutal survivors of the battle. Quite a short campaign, Isle of the Abbey could even be adapted into a one-off game if necessary.

DRAGONS

What would DUNGEONS & DRAGONS be without dragons? There are few creatures in the D&D bestiary more iconic than these powerful, innately magical beasts, who live for thousands of years, witnessing empires rise and fall from atop glittering hoards of treasure.

CHROMATIC DRAGONS

Traditionally, chromatic dragons represent the jealous, ego-driven side of dragonkind, and adventurers with any sense know to treat them with extreme caution. There are five types of chromatic dragon: black, white, red, blue, and green, each with different histories, cultures, and temperaments.

TIAMAT

The ancient, five-headed Dragon Queen, Tiamat, is the god of all evil dragons. Each of her five heads represents a different colour of chromatic dragon. Tiamat lives in Avernus, the first of the Nine Hells, and can obliterate entire armies in battle with her powerful breath weapons.

MINIONS & SERVANTS

Many chromatic dragons are served – willingly or not – by lesser creatures, either because these servants have fallen under their thrall, or because they seek a portion of the dragon's power. Kobolds and lizardfolk are often found working for dragons.

DRACONIC LAIRS

With little interest in humanoids, most chromatic dragons live in remote locations, away from prying eyes. Black dragons often make their lairs in swamps, while green dragons are commonly found in forests, and red dragons atop hills and mountains.

METALLIC DRAGONS

If chromatic dragons represent evil, metallic dragons represent wisdom and nobility. These wise dragons aim to preserve and protect the world and its life. Be wary, though – their memories are long, and they may hold you responsible for the actions of previous generations. There are five types of metallic dragon: bronze, brass, copper, silver, and gold.

BAHAMUT

In the Seven Heavens of the celestial plane lives the Platinum Dragon, Bahamut. On the rare occasions that this powerful deity ventures down to the Material Plane, he takes the form of a harmless-seeming human peasant, accompanied by seven ancient gold dragons disguised as canaries.

DRAGON KIN

There are many species in the Forgotten Realms that have dragon blood, including pseudodragons, dragonborn, and faerie dragons. There are also sorcerers with Dragon Ancestry, who gain their powers from ancestral contact with dragons.

SHAPE-SHIFTING

Some adult and ancient metallic dragons develop the ability to take on the form of various humanoids or other creatures. This allows the more curious among them to explore the world beyond their lairs, learning all they can about the world's empires, cultures, and communities.

BREATH WEAPONS

All dragons – metallic and chromatic – are innately magical, and have powerful elemental breath, which can be used as a weapon. The kind of element that a dragon can produce depends on its type: for example, bronze dragons breathe lightning, while brass dragons breathe fire.

DRAGON AGES

Dragons can live for thousands of years, growing in strength and power as they age. There are four stages of dragon life: baby dragons, known as wyrmlings, which are small and relatively weak, young dragons, adult dragons, and ancient dragons, which, at over 800 years old, are massively powerful.

INTELLIGENCE CHECK

1 **Which elves change their moods and abilities with the seasons?**
a. Wood elves
b. High elves
c. Drow
d. Eladrin

2 **What is the name of the only mountain in Icewind Dale?**
a. Kelvin's Cairn
b. Bryn Shander
c. Icespire Peak
d. Mount Hotenow

3 **Which two demiplanes are mirrors of the Prime Material Plane?**
a. The Astral Plane and the Ethereal Plane
b. The Feywild and the Shadowfell
c. Mount Celestial and the Nine Hells
d. The Plane of Earth and the Plane of Fire

4 **Where will you find the Gloaming and Summer Courts?**
a. Icewind Dale
b. The Feywild
c. Neverwinter Wood
d. The Underdark

5 **Which card from the Deck of Many Things allows you to erase one event from the past?**
a. Balance
b. Flames
c. Gem
d. The Fates

6 **When was the first edition of D&D created?**
a. 1964
b. 1974
c. 1984
d. 1994

7 **Which of these creatures is native to the world of Eberron?**
a. Firbolgs
b. Goliaths
c. Orcs
d. Warforged

8 **What is the challenge rating of the mighty tarrasque?**
a. 40
b. 20
c. 30
d. 50

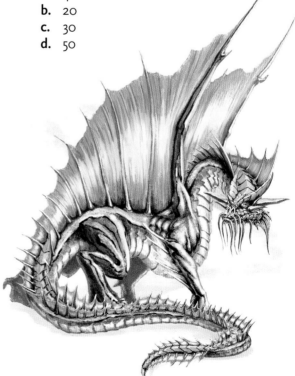

13 What is Menzoberranzan sometimes known as?
a. The Dark City
b. Castle Drizzt
c. Land of Lolth
d. City of Spiders

14 Eldritch Blast is a powerful cantrip cast by which magical class?
a. Warlock
b. Wizard
c. Sorcerer
d. Druid

15 What was the original name of the most famous beholder to take the name Xanathar?
a. The Eye
b. The Unyielding Sword
c. Misker the Pirate Tyrant
d. Blinky

16 In which Faerûn city does *Descent into Avernus* begin?
a. Neverwinter
b. Baldur's Gate
c. Waterdeep
d. Luskan

17 Who is the god of all evil dragons?
a. Bahamut
b. The Raven Queen
c. Tiamat
d. Tarrasque

18 Who is the witch Tasha's adoptive parent?
a. Vecna
b. Baba Yaga
c. Gandalf
d. Mordenkainen

19 What are the largest goblinoids?
a. Goblins
b. Hobgoblins
c. Bugbears
d. Kobolds

20 What class is the *Baldur's Gate III* character Shadowheart?
a. Wizard
b. Cleric
c. Fighter
d. Warlock

9 What species is Minsc's loyal companion Boo?
a. Miniature giant space hamster
b. Tiny war gerbil
c. Diminutive battle chinchilla
d. Pygmy capybara

10 Where does Neverwinter's year-round warmth come from?
a. Lava
b. Fire elementals
c. A second sun
d. Evocation magic

11 Which plane do Modrons hail from?
a. Mechanus, the Plane of Order
b. Pandemonium
c. The Abyss
d. The Astral Plane

12 What is the name of the vampire who killed Vecna?
a. The Raven Queen
b. The Lady of Pain
c. Kas the Bloody-Handed
d. Spooky Dave

ANSWERS ON PAGES 92-93 ›› **87**

GLOSSARY

A

ability – numerical characteristics that are used to determine success of actions. D&D has 6 core abilities: Charisma, Constitution, Dexterity, Intelligence, Strength and Wisdom.

ability score – a statistic that determines a character's adeptness in various areas.

actual play – a D&D game which is available to watch or listen to via livestream or podcast.

Armour Class (also AC) – a defensive stat based on a character's class and the armour they wear. Enemies must roll higher than this stat to complete an attack.

Arneston, Dave – co-creator of D&D.

B

barbarian – class of adept warriors that can channel rage to increase their strength.

bard – a musical class that use poems and songs to boost abilities and cast spells.

C

campaign – a pre-written adventure that has the basic storyline, puzzles, monsters and more for a party to journey through and explore.

cantrip – a basic spell that can be used without expending a spell slot.

challenge rating – a numerical indicator of the difficulty of an encounter or monster.

D

d20 – a dice with 20 numbered sides. There is also a d4, d6, d8, d10, d12 and d100.

drow – a dark elf.

druid – a class attuned with nature, and imbued with power from the natural world of deities.

D

Dungeon Master (also DM) – the person who leads the narrative of a campaign, sets up encounters, tasks players with puzzles and voices all the NPCs.

E

Eberron – a steampunk-style campaign setting populated by technological magic.

F

Faerûn – the most prominent continent in the Forgotten Realms.

fifth edition (also 5e) – the latest version of D&D.

fighter – a character class that specialises in the use of several weapons.

first edition – the original version of D&D.

Forgotten Realms – the most prominent setting in D&D, which focuses on high fantasy.

G

githyanki – a type of creature, hailing from the Astral Plane.

goblinoid – a type of creature, such as a goblin, bugbear or hobgoblin.

Gygax, Gary – co-creator of D&D.

H

hit points – indicator of a character's health. These are depleted as a character receives attacks.

I

initiative – the order in which combatants take their turn, determined by a dice roll at the start of battle.

inspiration – a gift from the DM to reward good roleplaying, can be used to aid rolls.

L

Lolth – the spider goddess who has corrupted Menzoberranzan.

M

modifier – a bonus score that you can add to certain rolls. Based on your ability scores.

monk – a class that is a master of martial arts and can channel magic through their ki.

N

Nine Hells – one of the outer planes, home to devils and demons.

NPC – a non-player character, voiced by the DM.

P

paladin – a class of holy soldiers, often highly armoured and able to use powerful weapons and magic.

party – the group of player characters that journey through a campaign together.

patron – an otherworldly deity or being that provides power and protection to warlocks, and occasionally whole parties.

Prime Material Plane – the primary plane where most campaigns will take place.

proficiency – a bonus modifier that is determined by your race or class.

R

ranger – a class of hunters that are adept at taking down monsters in the wild, often with a bow.

rogue – a class of dexterous, sneaky characters that often gravitate towards thievery and subterfuge.

roleplay – the act of assuming the role of a character, and making decisions through another's lens.

S

saving throw – a dice roll made in opposition to an attack or action, or to avoid death when unconscious.

skill – a characteristic, like acrobatics, which is determined by a character's ability score.

sorcerer – an often unpredictable magical class that can use powerful spells.

spell – a magic that can be performed in combat, either to aid allies or harm opponents.

subclass – a specialisation of a base class that has a more refined focus and extra skills.

U

Underdark, the – an underground region of the Forgotten Realms.

W

warlock – a class that gains their magical ability through pacts with mysterious beings.

wizard – a studious magic-wielding class with a wide range of spells and knowledge.

FAREWELL

Though there's no book in the world that could possibly hold all there is to know about the world of DUNGEONS & DRAGONS, we hope that this Annual will provide a taster of what this incredible game has to offer.

Now it's time to go out into the world and start playing! Whether you're starting your first game, searching for a new role-playing community, or a veteran player in the middle of a long-running campaign, there's always so much more to discover. Why not pick up one of the new campaigns or players' companions to refresh your gaming table? Plus, there are dozens of older campaigns, novels, games, and much, much more, just waiting for you to dive into and discover D&D's rich lore.

Let's get rolling ...

To keep up-to-date on the latest D&D news and entertainment, keep an eye on our official website, and follow us on social media.

DND.WIZARDS.COM
FACEBOOK.COM/DUNGEONSANDDRAGONS
TWITTER.COM/WIZARDS_DND
YOUTUBE.COM/USER/DNDWIZARDS
TWITCH.TV/DND
INSTAGRAM.COM/DNDWIZARDS/

ANSWERS

PAGE 14
Dungeon Crawl

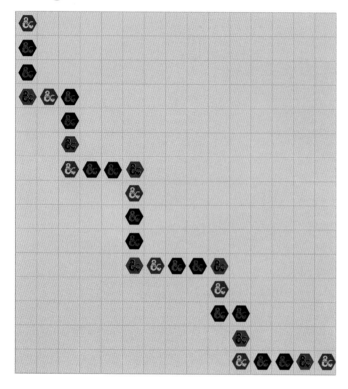

PAGE 15
Escape from Castle Ravenloft

Page 32
Volo's (Scrambled) Guide to Monsters

Tarrasque, Cloud Giant, Bronze Dragon, Pseudodragon, Smoke Mephit, Gelatinous Cube, Gibbering Mouther, Shambling Mound

PAGE 33
Pack It In

Rogue: crossbow, lesser healing, lockpick
Ranger: shortsword, potion of speed, rope
Fighter: warhammer, oil of slipperiness, grappling iron
Wizard: longbow, greater healing, candle

PAGE 44
Destination Search

J	H	N	S	A	L	T	M	A	R	S	H	X	N	K	U	E	B	R	Y	V	C	H	B	Z	N	W
K	E	I	D	M	E	O	Y	H	M	P	O	R	T	N	Y	A	N	Z	A	R	U	D	A	B	S	Y
E	D	H	E	M	T	G	F	G	N	P	M	T	K	R	I	E	O	C	Y	V	T	L	R	P	E	R
C	E	B	E	M	A	K	I	N	E	O	R	U	Y	T	E	R	A	E	A	C	A	U	E	D	E	M
Z	E	E	W	A	S	R	E	E	A	A	T	N	U	J	E	W	R	T	B	J	M	S	N	Z	J	S
H	B	B	O	J	L	O	L	Y	R	E	R	D	E	R	V	C	G	P	V	U	R	K	U	D	F	G
I	S	A	E	P	R	S	D	N	O	R	U	E	D	M	I	T	H	R	A	L	H	A	L	L	R	A
S	C	G	X	G	Z	R	S	E	I	E	N	R	F	A	D	R	E	F	T	S	R	N	R	A	O	T
P	G	F	R	D	A	U	O	H	B	N	V	D	B	S	N	S	O	S	M	N	B	N	G	D	R	E
I	V	B	O	I	M	N	F	Y	C	R	D	A	X	P	U	I	E	Q	W	S	A	E	D	F	G	M
N	X	C	E	R	E	G	S	X	A	P	O	R	I	Y	A	W	N	I	N	G	P	O	R	T	A	L
E	S	X	V	N	T	U	L	E	L	O	K	K	Y	H	G	A	F	R	E	L	E	O	D	R	Y	N
O	F	C	H	U	L	T	A	I	E	U	R	Y	S	N	Z	T	A	G	S	H	A	V	A	A	A	T
F	E	G	D	A	E	R	U	E	Q	D	L	I	O	K	I	E	U	O	Y	E	M	F	N	C	J	R
T	Y	H	E	G	R	Y	G	T	R	V	K	F	L	G	T	R	S	J	E	E	D	D	F	K	A	T
H	W	H	P	A	R	I	H	M	I	C	E	W	I	N	D	D	A	L	E	M	S	Y	U	L	I	Z
E	I	T	I	T	O	E	T	V	H	B	C	G	F	G	R	E	D	C	M	L	O	K	O	E	D	G
W	L	U	B	H	E	B	E	H	U	F	D	S	Y	T	N	E	K	S	L	R	M	R	N	S	V	E
O	D	F	D	A	R	Y	R	T	G	R	Z	E	Z	W	R	P	V	E	F	Z	D	S	W	S	R	P
R	S	M	K	S	O	R	U	E	J	H	G	R	F	E	T	G	R	U	E	Z	V	G	D	S	B	H
L	A	K	U	G	U	I	Z	N	E	D	E	R	Z	E	U	B	E	J	R	K	G	O	Z	E	Z	A
D	N	A	B	R	V	R	F	T	R	A	E	S	W	O	R	D	C	O	A	S	T	K	W	A	M	N
I	G	S	E	O	E	U	R	O	A	B	G	E	G	V	E	H	G	J	A	I	E	W	G	U	S	D
G	X	S	P	V	O	S	U	W	B	G	D	Z	S	S	E	G	B	A	K	Z	I	G	Y	J	B	A
T	G	R	E	E	I	U	J	N	A	G	N	E	V	E	R	W	I	N	T	E	R	B	E	H	E	L
E	S	S	I	A	G	S	E	S	B	E	U	G	V	S	G	E	R	S	C	G	X	S	I	A	H	I
M	G	P	E	Y	E	I	G	R	G	B	A	L	D	U	R	S	G	A	T	E	S	O	S	R	G	N

PAGE 45
Dice Disaster

The orange set has the d8 missing

PAGE 58
Perception Check

PAGE 59
Asking for Directions

5, 7, 6, 4, 8, 3, 9, 1, 2

PAGE 70
Siren's Call

1. Nothing
2. A mirror
3. His horse was named Friday
4. A river
5. A map
6. The letter E
7. A name

PAGE 71
A Fishy
Situation

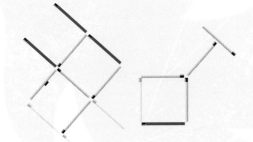

PAGE 78
Lost in the Crowd

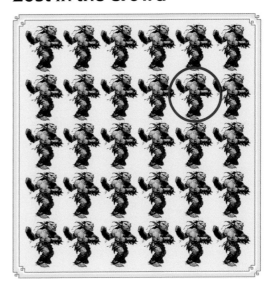

PAGE 79
X Marks the Spot

C 33

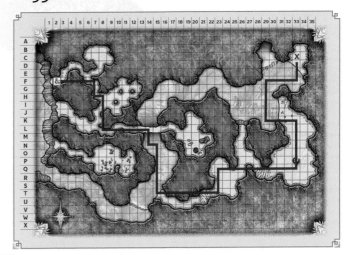

PAGE 86-87
Intelligence Check

1. d. Eladrin
2. a. Kelvin's Cairn
3. b. The Feywild and the Shadowfell
4. b. The Feywild
5. d. The Fates
6. b. 1974
7. d. Warforged
8. c. 30
9. a. Miniature giant space hamster
10. b. Fire elementals
11. a. Mechanus, the Plane of Order
12. c. Kas the Bloody-Handed
13. d. City of Spiders
14. a. Warlock.
15. a. The Eye
16. b. Baldur's Gate
17. c. Tiamat
18. b. Baba Yaga
19. c. Bugbears
20. b. Cleric